THE TOMORROW TOWER

JOHN MORALEE

The Tomorrow Tower

ISBN-13: 978-1517023751

ISBN-10: 1517023750

Visit www.**mybookspage.wordpress.com** to find out more about the author.

CONTENTS

THE TOMORROW TOWER

The bed was impossibly large, ten times the length of Iranda's body. She sat up and brushed the layers of pink silk from her face as she looked around for the first time. Her pillows followed the movement, supporting her gently in a comfortable position that caused the bed sheets to undulate and tingle with delightful static. She yawned and stretched. At the foot of the bed was a crystal balcony where five strangers floated on soft cushions. The strangers were two women and three men, all with their backs to her. They were wearing silver crowns and loose, diaphanous robes that left them almost naked, revealing their deeply tanned and well-toned bodies. They were looking out at the deep blue ocean and a patchwork of reefs far below.

"Where am I?" she asked.

No one replied.

Suddenly, five dolphins pirouetted out of the water in perfect formation. Their mirror-smooth skins shone in the sunlight, raining rainbows. At the peak of their leaps, the dolphins flicked their flippers, once, twice, three times, before returning beneath the waves with volcanic splashes. There, they chased a shoal of silver fish towards a large island on the horizon. Iranda had the impression that the people were in control of the dolphins. With clinical accuracy, the dolphins circled the shoal and moved in for food, one after the other, while the rest herded the silver fish.

Iranda could not remember this room. It was huge and very feminine, but also alien and not to her taste. Everything was a shade of pink, soft pink chairs and plush pink carpets competed to be pinker than the rest. Was it her room? She could not remember what she was doing here. And, worse, she could not remember the five people, though she was positive she knew them all intimately.

Something awful had happened.

Instinctively, she touched her abdomen. It was tender.

The five strangers removed their crowns and applauded each other for a magnificent game. Slowly, their cushions rotated to face the bed. One man noticed she was awake and grinned.

"Iranda! How do you feel?"

"Weak," she said.

The Tomorrow Tower

He floated across the room until he was above her. He stepped off the cushions and lay down beside her. Brushing the hair away from her eyes, he kissed her gently. His lips were warm and wet. She felt awkward.

"I should know you, shouldn't I?"

His smile vanished. "Iranda, I'm Kelsor. Kelsor - your lover."

The name meant nothing.

"You must remember?"

"No."

Kelsor looked at the others. "You said the pregnancy would work, Dison! No complications. Look, she doesn't even know me! What have you done?"

"I didn't know she would die," Dison said. "But look on the bright side - the replacement organs are working fine."

"But she lost the baby. And now her memory. How can she lose her memory? Tell me that!"

"Her neural implants will have saved her memories at the point of death. It's just a matter of adjustment." Dison paused. "I think."

"You think?"

"Nobody's tried a natural pregnancy in -"

"Eighteen thousand years," a woman said.

"Exactly, Helen. Eighteen thousand years. The knowledge was lost. Iranda accepted the risks before implantation, just like we all agreed. You can't blame me, Kelsor. It was your DNA we used for the father."

"Why can't I remember?" Iranda asked, but Kelsor and Dison

6

were having an argument that excluded her. It was as if she wasn't present.

"Her neural implants will unload their data into her repaired brain one neurone at a time," Dison said. "Sure, it may take a week or so for full memory recall, but it's not as if it is permanent."

Kelsor bit his lip. "Will she be able to have another baby?"

Dison shook his head. "Too dangerous."

This made Iranda sad. A baby, whatever that was, was the most important thing in the universe. It was soft and small and delicate and wonderful. And it was never to be. Dying meant nothing if she could have a baby.

Kelsor closed his eyes. Water seeped from his lids. There was a name for it, but she could not remember. "Iranda, what do you remember? Can you remember our names?"

She tried to think. She could remember dolphins were called dolphins, so the information could already be in her brain. Things were blurry, as though her past was there - but tantalisingly just out of reach. She looked at Kelsor and then at Dison and ... and there was a name coming. She could feel it ... and Helen and Eriqa ... and Morton. There were only six names to remember. Six humans left on Earth. Earth? The world. The planet. An image of a blue-white ball. Earth. She was remembering. "Yes, I know your names. I didn't, but now I do. When I remember something, it is as if I'd never forgotten. But it's hard, hard to think. Why is it hard to think, Kelsor?"

"That's to be expected. It's just a rewiring process. You must rest." He put his hands on her shoulder and gently urged her to lie down, but she resisted. She did not want to sleep. She had so much to remember.

"No," she said. "Please, I'm not tired. Not men - what's the word? - not in my head. Not *mentally*. I can't sleep. I'm ... hungry. Can I have some hunger, please?"

"Food, you mean. And the answer is, of course, yes."

*

The dining room was an exact replica of the Sistine Chapel, except for the sleek black dining table in its centre. Iranda sat next to Kelsor, who held her hand between courses and looked desperately into her eyes. The meal was languorous, a series of small courses of wafer-thin fish slices and delicate seaweeds with subtle flavours and textures that she ate slowly, relishing each dish. Every taste was a new sensation. The food was as fresh as could be, brought to the dining table in floating glass tanks by a man dressed in a long black jacket, black trousers, and a stiff white shirt. He was referred to as Butler. He cooked and prepared the food while they watched and chatted. He did not respond to her questions.

"My dear," Dison said, spinning a morsel of squid onto his fork, "he's not programmed for verbal communication. Butler can obey orders, but he's not a human, not like us. Ignore him. He's part of the furniture. The Tower controls him."

"Oh," she said, not understanding. Butler looked like them. She could not understand how he was like a table or chair.

Iranda learnt a lot during the sixteen courses. Her five

8

companions were eager to talk with the new stranger and provide a history lesson.

The place they lived in was simply called the Tower.

It was a luxurious survival shelter using self-repairing and self-evolving nanotechnological architecture. Machines as small as atoms formed any environment they desired. The Tower provided for their every desire by speech or thought-operated commands. It was a huge factory changing itself to their chosen configurations by absorbing whatever it needed from the mineral-rich ocean. It rose half a kilometre above the World Ocean, but most of it was beneath the water. Like an iceberg, Dison said. He sent an image of a big white thing to her neural implants. Beneath the water was a place called the Undercity. The Six did not go there, and when she asked why, they changed the subject. The Undercity was evidently an embarrassment. So she probed them more about the Tower.

The Tower was the only human-made structure to survive the Great Flood.

"What's the Great Flood?"

Kelsor told her that in the distant past there had been continents, massive areas of land above the water where millions and millions of people had lived. There were no visual records, but Iranda could imagine them. Wonderful places. Now there was nothing but water.

There had been a global accident.

An ice comet had hit the Earth on somewhere called America, wiping out most of the Earth's population in one orbit-shifting cataclysm. As a result of the shorter orbit and input of billions of tonnes of ice, sea levels had risen kilometres in as many days. The continents submerged. For the survivors, there were few choices. Some left for space, and nobody knew what had happened to them. Some tried to live on the surface in ships and on floating artificial islands - reefcities - but the World Tides proved too dangerous and they soon perished. The rest created Undercity.

Iranda probed her friends, eking out information bit by bit, byte by byte.

Undercity was a haven for the refugees of the Great Flood. It had been built so the survivors could survive for millennia under the water, waiting for the sea levels to fall so they could reclaim the land. The theory was all they had to do was wait for the sea level to fall. But the society of wildly different cultures and religions, packed together in such a small space, soon fractured and fought a thousand-year war. The Six isolated themselves against the in-fighting by living in the Tower and preventing anyone else from entering. They had lived many thousands of years in isolation, kept alive by their internal nanotechnological repair systems and the Tower's defence network. Now the Tower was once again above the water. They were free to repopulate the Earth.

"What happened to the rest of the people?"

"That's not dinner conversation," Helen said.

"I'll show you later," Kelsor promised. "Maybe tomorrow."

Finishing the meal, Iranda felt as if she could eat another, but she did not want to wait another two hours for all the courses. Why could they not just put it all on one plate and be done with it?

To relearn about herself, Kelsor suggested she visit the library. So Iranda wandered through the vast halls of the tenth level. Ancient books and CDs and DVDs and VR hardware stacked the shelves ... The collected works of aeons. It was all new to her. She gorged on information, revelling in the learning process, needing to know, needing to imagine. And as she did so, her neural implants made connections, clarifying and expanding. She could have spent a thousand years in the library, but then Kelsor returned and asked her if she wanted to see the roof garden.

"Yes, please."

They left the library, walked through an atrium filled with pre-Great Flood art, then boarded a glass elevator. They stopped at two floors, picking up the others.

"Tower," Dison said, "take us to the roof."

"Yes, Mr Dison."

"Who was that?" Iranda asked.

Helen and Eriqa laughed. Dison said: "That's the Tower's personality. You can talk to it if you want anything. It's not a true AI - they are too dangerous - but it does provide whatever we need."

"Hello, Tower," Iranda said, embarrassed. Why couldn't she remember these things?

"Welcome back, Miss Iranda. How are you feeling?"

"Great," she replied.

The elevator rose. When the doors opened, Iranda gasped at the view. The roof garden was really a vast park on the top of the tower, dark green Douglas firs sweeping away into the distance. It was as dense as a jungle in places. A sandy path led the way like a river of butter. Dison led the way, naming the plants. He plucked a banana from an overhanging branch and handed it to Iranda. It was sweet. Soon palm trees heavy with coconuts mixed with weeping willows and giant redwoods, a jigsaw puzzle of climates in just a few acres. Iranda could hear a waterfall and the chatter of birds and insects high up in the swollen canopy. She followed the others through a garden filled with parakeets and butterflies and buzzing bees; then the trees thinned, unveiling the stone wall at the edge of the tower and an ebony staircase. She climbed the staircase until she was above the forest canopy on a transparent platform that revealed the full extent of the roof garden.

"I thought everything was wiped out in the Great Flood."

"Everything was on the surface," Dison said. "But the Tower stored DNA samples of every species for repopulating the Earth. The gene bank contains billions of lifeforms, from whales down to viruses. It's taken a thousand years to get this ecosystem online, but it's worth it, yes?"

"Yes."

Iranda ran to the platform's edge. Below, the World Ocean was a myriad of blues and greens, dotted with verdant reef-islands. A sprawling archipelago abundant with life. The sun was directly overhead, warm and comforting, glinting off the water like diamonds and sapphires. She had been here before, many times. It was home.

The Tomorrow Tower

A soft hissing caught her attention.

She spun around and saw six mirrored parasols growing out of the ground. The parasols quickly shaded six wicker chairs, also grown from basic molecules as she watched with wonder. Butler ascended from the forest with six crowns in his hands.

"Kelsor, what are those crowns for? I saw them the other day and -"

"Do as I do," Kelsor said, pulling her towards a chair. It was comfortably moulded to her own shape.

Kelsor took the chair next to hers. Butler placed a crown on his head and stepped back. Kelsor closed his eyes and his body slackened.

Seeing the others do the same, Iranda waited until Butler arrived with her crown. The crown was surprisingly light. Once it rested on her scalp, there was a shift in perception. As well as being in her own body, she was also outside it, looking down. Iranda, on the chair, looked up and saw a silver glimmer in the air. She could see herself from the glimmer's position, a full panoramic view. She could hear voices. The Six. Kelsor's voice was in her mind saying the thing she was looking at was called a sprite.

A sprite?

Yes. It's an empathic machine. Close your eyes and detach completely from your body, become the sprite.

I don't know how!

Just do it.

She closed her eyes. Instantly, the layer of herself in her body

13

vanished.

Now she was the sprite.

Five sprites joined her position above the sleeping people. She could see the sprites clearly, little bug-like machines with lights flickering across their pearl-textured surfaces. She could see and hear, but she felt nothing. They were in direct communication with her.

What am I?

You are in transition. Iranda, follow us. When you see what we do, you'll understand.

One by one, the sprites set off over the roof and down on the air current towards the ocean. She trailed after them, propelled by nanotech engines in her wings.

The water ahead sparkled.

Dolphins?

Yes.

The sprites were sleek torpedoes honing towards the dolphins. The sprites parted company and crashed into the dolphins and merged, all except Iranda. She was reluctant.

Choose one, Kelsor urged.

Iranda selected the nearest. Spinning, flying, she hit the dolphin's grey flank, half-expecting herself to be destroyed by the impact. But the contact was wet and pliant, and in a moment she was inside the dolphin's blood. Instinctively, she swam upstream. There was a map in her head, of arteries and veins. She headed for the brain. In a matter of microseconds, she latched on. Her body detonated, sending femtotech machines in all directions.

Awareness blossomed like a supernova.

She was the dolphin.

It was incredible. Iranda had total control and total experience. Her mind filled with the strange but beautiful shapes of echolocation. To see with sound was dizzyingly awesome. A part of her head - the melon - sent high-pitched clicks out into the environment, bouncing off the surface, and other dolphins, forming a clear picture that complemented her vision. The experience was so vivid that she floundered, but reborn memories bubbled up from her neural implants and took over the autonomic processes. She was swimming through the clear water, her skin adapting to the feel of the it, as soft as a lover's caress. A deep red reef was ahead, scintillating with life.

Race you, Kelsor thought to her.

She watched the dolphins accelerate, their flippers and tails sending a colourful turbulence behind them. She chased them, marvelling at how natural being a dolphin felt. She was born to live like this. The reef grew larger ... and she overtook Helen and Dison. Eriqa and Morton swam parallel for thirty seconds, but a burst of energy sent her past them. Kelsor was almost at the reef. She could hear him laughing, and it was then she realised she was laughing. This was so much fun!

And Kelsor reached the reef one second before she did. But it did not matter, for the race had been the pleasure, not the winning. Iranda rushed to the surface, breaking free in a white spray of dancing droplets. She cried out in pleasure, with the sound coming out as a series of ultrasonic clicks. Then, after taking a joyous breath, she somersaulted and plunged into the foaming water.

An hour later, exhausted in pleasure, Iranda circled slowly.

How do we do this?

The sprite links into the brain of any creature of sufficient intelligence, Dison answered. He seemed to be more interested in the scientific explanations than the others. *You are really on remote experience. What you feel as another creature is in your own brain, back in the Tower. The sprite provides a link and translates into the human sensorium. You can be any creature with a respectable neural network. Dolphins are excellent because they have large brains, so are sharks and -*

Why don't we just show her? Kelsor said, sounding irritated. *Iranda, retract the sprite from the dolphin.*

She was reluctant to do so; it felt too good, but once she had thought it, then it happened automatically. She said goodbye and was outside, floating in the water like the zooplankton. The dolphin continued swimming as if nothing had happened.

Her sprite had collated into its basic form. The lack of sensations was stifling. It was like being in a room with no doors or windows. She craved to be inside the dolphin's mind again, but she watched it swim away, to do whatever dolphins did when not under control.

Kelsor's sprite orbited her.

Down, Iranda. Go deeper and down.

Just the two of them left the surface far behind until the water changed from green to blue to black. The sprite had radar and echolocation, but these systems were basic compared with the dolphin's. The water bustled with fish, moving in chaotic patterns. There was something big below, no, two somethings. The sprite enhanced optical sensitivity. She could see a white shape mottled with black. As she approached, she realised the blackness was a covering of large barnacles on a white surface. The barnacles were riding on the back of a humpback whale.

And then she was that humpback whale.

The humpback whale was pregnant.

*

When Iranda opened her own eyes, the sky was tinged with pink clouds. The sun was orange and close to the horizon.

There was a dull pain in her stomach. No, it wasn't real. A phantom pain for a phantom pregnancy. She removed the crown and walked stiffly to the staircase, followed by Kelsor.

"Didn't you enjoy today?"

"Yes," she said.

"What's wrong?"

"The whale was pregnant," she said.

"Oh, I'm sorry." Kelsor held her then, and they cried together. Minutes later, they were in the pink bedroom, making love. The massive bed did not seem large enough for all the positions they tried. Iranda tried to purge herself of grief for the baby that never was. Afterwards, Iranda looked into Kelsor's eyes. "People used to have babies, didn't they?"

"All the time."

"So why can't we?"

"Living above the water has problems. Before the atmosphere repaired itself, the cosmic radiation made us sterile and damaged our cells. Our nanotech keeps us alive forever, but reproduction is ... complicated. Our nanotech thinks of it as an infection. Dison's worked on the problem for centuries, and we'd thought we'd cracked it, but ... but it failed. I'm sorry."

"Don't be sorry," she said. "At least we tried."

*

The tinkle of metal woke her. Butler was standing at the bed, holding a silver tray weighed down by a china tea service. Iranda was alone in the bed. Sunlight streamed through the windows. "What time is it?"

Butler did not reply. The Tower did.

"A quarter to noon, Miss Iranda."

"What is Butler doing here?"

"You always drink tea now, Miss Iranda. Butler is merely following your instructions."

"I don't want tea, whatever it tastes like," she said. Butler bowed and removed himself from the room. "Tower, where is Kelsor?"

"Mr Kelsor is presently in the Game Room. He's expecting you

The Tomorrow Tower

at one o'clock. Your shower and clothes are ready."

*

The Game Room was just above sea level, at a level inaccessible by elevator. She had to walk down several flights of stairs, then through an archway. It was a vast room that filled an entire floor of the tower. Presently, it was a replica of the St Peter's Basilica. (Roman Catholic architecture was Helen's favourite style, and the Tower had decorated the Game Room to suit her taste.) Iranda's footsteps echoed eerily as she joined the group in the room's centre. They were already wearing their crowns. The kings and queens of the new world. The air above was filled with a shimmering cloud of sprites, nebulous and milky. The Six stood around a dark, square hole in the floor. The shaft looked endless.

"How much do you remember this morning?" Dison asked dreamily. Iranda was aware that he wasn't all in his mind. He was joined to a sprite.

"A little more," she said. "I know this room. We go here often."

"She is remembering," Helen said. "I wonder if she can remember how to play the game."

"I hope not," Eriqa said. "Otherwise you don't stand a chance, darling."

"What's the game?" Iranda asked.

Morton answered, speaking in his manic stutter. An emerging memory told her he was painfully shy and usually allowed Eriqa to do the talking for him. But the game was his passion, the one thing that mattered in his life. "The g-g-game! You c-can't beat the g-game. The g-game of life. And d-death. And love. Y-you c-can't beat the game."

"Shut up, darling," Eriqa said.

Morton looked down at his shoes.

"Put on your crown," Kelsor said to Iranda.

They sat in a row, holding hands. The floor produced wooden pews to hold their bodies.

Now she was simultaneously a sprite in the cloud, looking down at the hole, and herself. A ripple of a new emotion gripped her. Fear?

Are we going to be dolphins today?

Darling, you have forgotten, haven't you?

The game? What are the rules?

No rules.

So what do we do?

Play until one wins.

Leaving herself behind, she detached from the sprite cloud and flew towards the hole. The way was lit by the five sprites in front. The shaft was part of the old elevator, the elevator that used to go all the way down to the Undercity. Gravity was the master of the descent. It took all of her concentration to control the flight. A kilometre zoomed by, the shaft a featureless nowhere. Then the shaft branched and branched again.

There was light coming from somewhere below, crimson light.

The Tomorrow Tower

She could feel the photons brushing against her sprite's shields.

She saw an opening.

She entered a vast cavern of some sort. The red light came from strip lights running the length of the ceiling. The room was really too large to be considered an indoor environment. It felt like an open space filled with metallic stalactites and stalagmites. A black sea of oil surrounded islands built of junk. Rust and corrosion had eaten away at the buildings, forming a metal landscape of jagged and fluted edges.

The Undercity, she thought.

Wrecked and ruined buildings stretched for as far as her sprite could see. Here the nanotech had failed and decay set in. There were fires at street level and the blue-white lightning of electricity conduits arcing across kilometres.

And there were people.

She could see them now.

Dirty, filthy people. Thousands of them, squatting in doorways, huddled together in groups, some sitting alone ... All surrounded by rubbish.

She saw the other sprites enter five people.

As she hovered over the group, an old man waved at her, dressed in grey and brown rags. His teeth were missing or yellow. "Come on, Iranda. It's me, Kelsor. Pick a person."

I don't want to do it. I don't want to do it. It's not right. It's not right.

But she accidentally slapped into the back of a girl's head -

- and before she could pull out, she was a fourteen-year-old

The Tomorrow Tower

called Nandy G.

Immediately, Nandy's memories were available. Nandy was the fourth daughter of Jem G, who was dead. Nandy had seen Gorf C, her cousin, rape and kill her mother - after the light in the sky entered him two weeks ago. She had been unable to sleep since, fearing the lights.

I am the light, Iranda thought, horrified.

The old man inhabited by Kelsor called the Six together. "Iranda, the game is to be the last survivor. I've sent a code so your sprite can't pull out until either you die, or all of us are dead."

"It's the ultimate challenge," Morton said, through the body of a dark-haired man.

"I don't want to play this game," Iranda said weakly.

"Fine," Helen/a fat man said, "it's your life."

Iranda/Nandy ran.

*

She was hiding in a damp basement when Morton found her. He'd picked up an iron pipe on his travels, and his face was smeared with another's blood.

"N-naughty, n-naughty, little girl," he said, "you can't hide in the Undercity. N-not for long."

He broke her arms, then beat Nandy until she could no longer scream. Iranda tried to fight back, but Morton's man was too strong. He hit Nandy's skull with three vicious cracks that dazed her. Still,

The Tomorrow Tower

Nandy was alive, but barely. Morton sneered as he raped her. Nandy's sad life flooded into Iranda as minutes felt like hours. Morton was raping her too, albeit indirectly. For every day of Nandy's life, she had lived in terror of this day.

For Iranda, it was a relief when Morton ended Nandy's life.

*

Iranda opened her eyes in the Game Room. She could still feel Morton's fingers pressed into her throat, but the feeling passed as she rubbed her skin. There were no bruises on her body. She looked at the Six, terrified by her experience. Helen and Kelsor were not present, presumably they were already out of the game, but Morton, Dison and Eriqa remained entranced.

Morton was smiling.

Iranda shook off the crown and staggered towards the elevator, vomiting all of the way.

*

Iranda looked down from the balcony. The archipelago did not look so beautiful now, or so new to her eyes. As the old Iranda's memories added to her childlike brain, there were changes to her personality that she could feel. Soon, she knew, she would not care about the view. It was all the same. Every day was a repeat of the last. Maybe the weather changed, but there was nothing she had not done. Yesterday's ride as a dolphin could never be repeated; every nuance was familiar. She needed the intensity of feelings that the sick game produced. Basic emotions, like fear and anger and pain, were the addiction of an immortal soul seeking oblivion, not life, but her mind had been too cluttered to see it before.

Perhaps she was naive to believe there was another way to live, but she wanted to act now before she became that jaded woman again, the Iranda incapable of caring. In an unexpected way, her pregnancy had created a new life. But how long could it last?

She did not hear Kelsor approach until he touched her arm. She flinched.

"About the game," he said. "I had no idea that would upset you. You must have picked a bad character. It can happen."

"It was horrible. Disgusting. I never want to do that again."

"But the game was your idea."

"That," she said, "was not my idea."

"It was. You'll soon remember. You invented it, to relieve the infernal boredom."

She could feel the phantom pregnancy again. She did not want to become the Iranda everyone knew and loved, the selfish creature lurking inside her neural implants. Not if the Nandys of the Undercity had to suffer for her entertainment.

"Why? Why do we keep those people down there?"

"They're worse than animals. They caused the war that forced us to live in the Tower. They destroyed their own nanotechnology. We are the keepers of peace, maintaining a stable existence, but they have become ... well, you saw how they live. They have such brief lives they learn nothing. Anyway, they can't complain. We send down enough food and power for their needs."

They live that way because of us, she thought. "Butler's one of them, isn't he?"

Kelsor nodded. "He managed to find a way up through the levels. Quite impressive, for an Undercity creature. He crawled up the shaft. The Tower informed us, so we gave the Tower sprite control over him rather than killing him."

"We made him a slave?"

"If he'd been allowed to roam free, he could have done untold damage. Look, this will all become clear in a few days. You're not fully you, yet. You don't understand what it's like to live like this, just the six of us in the entire world. You have to make sacrifices."

But we make them live like that, she thought. She could not share her thoughts with Kelsor, she did not entirely trust him. He believed in the status quo. *We're afraid to let them out. They have nothing. We have everything, but we abuse our powers.*

"What are you thinking?"

"Nothing. I'm just remembering."

"The others are expecting us for dinner."

*

Iranda brooded throughout the meal. What was she going to do? If she did nothing, then the old Iranda would return. She did not want that. She could hardly talk honestly with her so-called friends. All they talked about was the game, and how their strategies had worked or not. It was depressing. Life was a game to them, something to score points on. And humans, like Butler and Nandy, were their playthings.

Iranda could barely taste the minuscule portions. When the last course arrived, she just had to look at it to know that she could not eat it. There was something wrong with it. She had seen it before.

"Please, tell me, what is this?"

"Dolphin, of course."

"Dolphin." The word stung. She pushed her plate aside. "Everyone, please excuse me. I don't feel well."

"It must be the data transference," Dison said. "It'll pass."

She stood up. The room swayed.

"Do you want me to come with you?" Kelsor asked.

"No. Enjoy the dinner."

She left the room, but she stayed near the door, listening. She could hear Dison: "I say we reboot her neural implants. It's obvious she isn't the same Iranda."

Kelsor said: "We have to give the process time. Another day - see if she's feeling better."

"No improvements and we reboot, agreed?"

"Agreed," sighed Kelsor.

Iranda slipped away to her room. She was shaking.

New memories changed her perspective on her relationship with Kelsor.

The Tomorrow Tower

She did not love him and never had. They were not lovers out of an emotional bond, but because it was something to do. During her time in the Tower, she'd had sexual relationships with each one of the six, often more than one at a time. Presently, they were in a century of heterosexual monogamy, but, in the past, the six had explored all permutations. It was merely Kelsor's turn to be her partner.

We can't even be true to ourselves, she realised. *No wonder we take out our frustrations on other life. We behave like the gods of the Greeks and Romans. And, like those gods, our time has passed. It's time for a change.*

Worse, she had not wanted a baby to love and nurture, but to provide entertainment as a new companion for the six. Another plaything.

She lay down on her bed and tore the sheets apart.

*

Later, when Kelsor came to her room to make love, she turned him away with excuses. Luckily, he did not press the matter. He did not get a chance to see the torn sheets.

Once he was gone, Iranda wandered onto the balcony to watch the stars pop out of the midnight blue sky. The Milky Way was a sliver of luminosity. There were people out there doing what humans were born to do, to expand and explore. To be the best they could be. A cool breeze made her skin goosebumpy. Shivering, she returned inside.

The Tomorrow Tower

She wondered if dolphins mourned their dead.

"Tower, where is Butler?"

"Butler is in a sleep cycle, Miss Iranda. Shall I wake him?"

"No," she said. "But I want you to take my instructions."

"It will be my pleasure, Miss Iranda."

"Are the others sleeping?"

"Yes."

"Good. In six hours, I want you to instruct Butler to build a ladder from equipment in the storage deck. He must put the ladder down the shaft into the Undercity. You must use him to bring people to the tower. You will then release sprite control."

"I must state that this action could be a danger to the Six."

"I know, but that won't matter if things work out right."

"Miss?"

"Just follow instructions, Tower. This is a level zero command."

"Understood, Miss Iranda. Does this mean Butler will not be making breakfast?"

"Yes. No more breakfasts, Tower. In six hours you will answer to only the people from the Undercity. You will function as a teacher and arbitrator. You must show them how to use the library and help them adapt to the surface world." She paused. Was that all she wanted to say? No. "One more thing. At that time, you must also destroy all sprites that are not being used by the Six and erase the knowledge of how to build new ones. In the meantime, Butler has to do one more thing."

Tower listened to her instructions.

The Tomorrow Tower

The Game Room was dark at first, but Tower lit the ceiling with enough light to illuminate the centre. Iranda crossed the floor, stopping at the hole. She collected the crowns together. Then she placed one on her head and took control of a sprite. She directed the sprite up the tower, to the bedroom of Dison and Helen. They were sleeping. She sneaked inside Dison's unconscious mind. She briefly examined his memory, discovering that his thoughts were cold and mechanistic. His repopulation of the planet wasn't for altruistic reasons, but for entertainment and egotism. Any humanity had been washed away centuries ago.

Back in the chamber, she removed the crown. The sprite was left inside Dison, but he would not be aware of it if he woke. Iranda repeated the action for Helen, then went to Milton and Eriqa. Next, she sent a sprite to Kelsor's bedroom. The bed was unmade, but he wasn't in the room. Concerned, she flew into the bathroom. It was empty. She returned to the bedroom, flew around it, then went out onto the balcony. He wasn't taking a midnight walk -

Abruptly, she lost the transmission.

*

Kelsor had lifted the crown from her head. "Iranda, what's going on? I couldn't sleep, so I went back to your room, but you weren't

29

there. What are you doing down here?"

"I ... wanted to practise the game."

"Oh," he said, yawning, "that's a good idea. Get back to your old form, huh?"

She nodded.

"I don't suppose you want to -" He stopped, puzzled. "Iranda, why are you holding all the crowns?"

She saw the flash of understanding on his face. He shouted, "No!" as she raised the next crown. He was still reaching for it as she entered a sprite. Under her control, the sprite dived out of the cloud towards Kelsor. He turned and tried to swat it. It was a mistake. He should have just taken the crown off her head. The sprite passed between his fingers and entered his cheek. He slapped himself, but it did no good. Iranda's sprite buried through tissue and bone, then entered his bloodstream. Quickly, it entered his brain.

The sprite exploded, taking control.

Iranda wasted no more time. She forced Kelsor to return to his room and sleep before she removed her control. Taking the last unused crown, she selected a sprite and sent it into her own head. Instantly, it was as if there were double the thoughts, a continuous deja vu.

Butler emerged from the shadows. He removed the crown from her head. She gave him the crowns and watched him go to the stairs. He would now place the crowns in order while she went back to her room. The first crown would go on Dison and so on until everyone was wearing one.

The Tomorrow Tower

Iranda watched the stars fade and the sun rise, the blossoming of a new day, then returned to her bed. She was tired, tired of living. The old Iranda was coming back.

Butler entered with her crown.

"Are you sure about this?" Tower asked.

"Yes."

Butler placed it on her head.

A loop was created.

She controlled Dison, who controlled Eriqa, who controlled Helen, who controlled Milton, who controlled Kelsor, who controlled her. If she sent the code Kelsor had sent to her sprite during the game, then they would be trapped in a null circuit, with nobody able to act under their own volition.

She was scared. She did not want to do it. She knew that if she sent the code, then the loop would be permanent and Butler would hide their bodies somewhere the new inhabitants of the Tower would never find. And as long as the crowns were on their heads, they would be unable to interfere with life. They would be immortal, but harmless. She had to do it for human life to be reborn. She sent the code.

The Six were trapped in the loop.

Iranda's game was over, but humanity could live again.

The sun shone into the bedroom as Butler walked away.

He had a ladder to build.

REHAB

Mom was crying on the phone, trying to get the words out between asthmatic gasps. I clutched the phone, wishing to God that I could read the letter myself. "Mom, take it slower. What's happened?"

"It's Frank. They've found him."

I looked out of the window at Vanessa sunning herself on the patio, then closed the glass doors so I could think without the traffic noise. My heart hammered. My brother had been MIA for ten years and I'd accepted he was dead, but now the thought of his body being recovered twisted my stomach in knots. "Mom, I'm listening. Go on."

"They found him in the Kabistan delta two months ago ... and he's alive."

Her tone wasn't good, like I expected. There was something more she had to say. "That's great, isn't it?"

"Michael, the people say ... they say ... they say he was a deserter."

"What?" I couldn't hear her for the pounding in my ears. "Frank was a patriot. Hell! He volunteered!"

The Tomorrow Tower

I heard Mom wince at 'hell.'

"Mom, what people are you talking about?"

"The army people. They had a trial and all," she said. "Michael, they've put him in one of those VA Rehab places in Santa Barbara. They did some kind of mind scan or something."

She paused.

I could imagine her looking at the photographs of Frank in his uniform the day before he shipped out. "The letter says he's coming home in two days, but I'm afraid of what they've done to him. Can you come home?"

"Of course," I said. "I'll just have to explain things to Vanessa."

*

Vanessa insisted on coming with me, despite my warning about East LA. I drove the Kev-Chev carefully, avoiding stopping at intersections if I could. The Chevrolet's Kevlar plating offered excellent protection against drive-by shootings, but we were both edgy. Vanessa sat low in the passenger seat as we passed through the graffiti and bullet-damaged neighbourhoods, nudging me each time she saw a man wearing a bandanna.

"He doesn't have to be a gangsta," I said.

"Yeah, right. I'll write that on your tombstone."

The gang warfare just reminded me why I'd gone to Boston. I'd seen a lot - maybe too much - living here as a kid. Now my old neighbourhood was popular for shootings and jaz dealing and not much else.

"This is home," I said, turning the corner of 8th and Lincoln.

There were new corrugated metal sheets over the windows of Mom's house. Security cameras followed our movements. Mom didn't want to live in a retirement village way out in the suburbs, like I'd suggested, so she had made the place up as a fortress. I got out and looked up and down the street, watching the steam rise from the sidewalks. There was no one around - but I could hear casual gunfire and dogs barking and screaming sirens.

Vanessa joined me, holding my hand, squeezing. "Nice place. Shame about the people."

"Don't say that to my Mom, okay?"

Vanessa glared at me as if to say: "What have you got me into?"

The truth was, I didn't know.

Mom opened the front door. "Michael, don't leave your car on the street."

"You don't have a garage, Mom."

She considered that as if it were *my* fault. Then she looked at Vanessa, then back at me. "Is it insured?"

"Yes - it's a rental."

"Well, forget it. Are you two coming in or waiting for a bullet?"

"I'll get the suitcases," I said, entering the shrine to Frank.

Sure enough, on the top of the living room's 3DTV was a picture of Frank, beaming at the camera. Mom had already prepared for Frank's homecoming by rearranging the furniture. Vanessa and I sat on the sofa and listened to my mother tell us how glad she was to have company, how she didn't often get many visits since my father died, and how she didn't get out a lot with the crime going on. She made feel guilty for living and bored Vanessa enough to get her to unpack the clothes upstairs.

"Come in the kitchen, Michael."

Mom had baked a cake several tiers high. It looked like some kind of homage to weddings, coated with inches of icing, whipped cream and chocolate flakes. The words 'Welcome Home, Frank' were written in edible silver beads that you could break your teeth on. "You think he'll like it?"

"Uh, he'll love it."

She started crying. As I was hugging her, she asked me if I was going to marry *that* girl.

"We're living together," I said.

"A ring on her finger wouldn't look so bad, Michael." She went to the stove and carried out a tray of heart-shaped cookies. "Double chocolate chip - Frank's favourite."

"Mom, Frank's nearly thirty. He liked those when he was a kid."

"He's never too old for cake and cookies," she said.

I didn't argue because I saw the magic in her eyes. Her other son was coming home. It was a reason for celebrating.

"I want him to have the best party in the world," she said.

For the rest of the day, the three of us decorated the living room with streamers and Christmas stuff pulled from the dusty boxes in the basement. Soon everything glittered. Then we cleaned the furniture and vacuumed (something usually reserved for the day

The Tomorrow Tower

before Thanksgiving.)

I arranged for Frank's high-school buddies (twenty in all) to arrive just before noon tomorrow.

Rehab would bring Frank to the door at around one o'clock.

*

Out of all of Frank's high-school buddies, only eight kept their promise. A couple had died of natural causes, one had OD'd on jaz, and the others just didn't bother coming. A few relatives and some old ladies from the LA Evangelical Christian Church made up the numbers. Of Frank's friends, I only remembered Garcia and Styles - they'd hung out with Frank before he joined the Marines. They both looked like they had fallen on hard times. They seemed more interested in the prospect of free food than a reunion of classmates. Mom welcomed them like they were members of our family. I watched them so they didn't steal anything.

At noon the proximity alarm bleeped. I rushed to open the door, half-expecting Frank to be standing there wearing a chest of medals and a big grin. But it was an hour early.

It was a captain dressed in his uniform with his chest covered with medals. "I'm Captain Robert Andowitz."

We shook hands. I'd never heard of him. The confusion must have shown on my face, because he quickly continued.

"I was Frank's commanding officer at the battle of Tai Fo."

"Oh, right. I heard about that," I said. "Didn't they use gene weapons against you?"

"Yes, it was hell. A lot of good men died. Or worse."

Andowitz stared into space for a minute, then looked uneasily at his polished boots. "Well, Frank saved my life that day. When I heard he'd been found, I had to see if he was okay. Is he in?"

"He hasn't arrived yet. Come in."

"Thanks."

Andowitz relaxed his military posture over a couple of Buds.

"I don't believe Frank deserted, despite what they said. I was at the trial. One big sham, you ask me. There was Frank, sort of drugged-up, unable to talk, and the prosecutor was asking these questions and ... I just don't believe it. When he went missing, they didn't lift a finger to find him, but when he turns up, *then* they take an interest. Hell, they probably just made up the charges to get a volunteer for Rehab."

I asked him about the war. Andowitz said that Frank had been called back to HQ shortly after the bombing of Tai Fo. Promoted to Special Forces, just like that. Since his promotion, Andowitz had not heard from Frank. Andowitz told me that once his present tour ended next month, he would quit the army, even though he was near to becoming a major. "It's all politics. A guy is left for ten years behind enemy lines because of a screw-up, but Washington would rather call him a traitor than admit they let him down. It's Afghanistan all over again. I can't be a part of that."

The front door's proximity alarm bleeped again.

Mom rushed out of the kitchen. "It's him! It's Frank!"

The Tomorrow Tower

A black ambulance stopped at the end of the driveway. As I stepped out to welcome Frank, two men in black suits stepped out of the cab and blocked my path. I heard Andowitz swear behind me. A third Rehab man stopped Mom from approaching the vehicle.

"M'am, step back. This is government property."

I didn't like his tone, like an IRS inspector.

"Is Frank in there or what?"

"Everyone step back. This is government property."

The rear doors flipped open. The Rehabs went around and lifted a man onto the sidewalk.

He was in a wheelchair.

This man looked at me, straight eye to eye, and I wanted to cry. This thing couldn't be my brother, not Frank. This man was all skin and bones. His eyes were a sickly yellow. His hands were almost transparent, nails gnarled and blackened. I'd seen the effects of gene weapons on TV, but never so close, so real, so terrible.

Mom fainted.

Andowitz grabbed her before she hit the ground. "I'll take her inside."

I looked at the stranger in the wheelchair. They'd made a mistake. He wasn't Frank. It was a stranger.

"That isn't my brother," I said.

The Rehabs ignored my comment.

"That can't be Frank! He looks like a zombie! That is not my brother."

I felt Vanessa's hand in mine.

The Tomorrow Tower

"Yes it is," she said, quietly.

Gravity doubled, and I felt my knees weakening. Vanessa held me upright while I kept staring, staring at the wheelchair.

"The wheelchair is not permanent," one Rehab employee said. "It's just a legal requirement. Before we hand over the patient, someone will have to pay his medical fees."

"Medical fees?" I said.

"They total sixty-four-thousand dollars."

"What? That's outrageous. How am I supposed to pay that?"

"We accept credit cards," the man said.

I wanted to punch him. "I'm not giving you blood-suckers that."

"I'll pay," Andowitz said. "Least I can do."

"No," I said. I calmed myself down with a deep breath. "I will. But thanks for offering."

Andowitz looked hurt, but he said nothing.

I paid and signed for Frank like a piece of property. One Rehab looked at me with the coldest look I've ever seen. I don't know what he had against me. Maybe it was for being a human being. Maybe it was for calling him a blood-sucker. I don't know. Just looking at him gave me a nasty taste in my mouth.

I approached the wheelchair with Vanessa telling me to stay calm. The stranger's head moved, and I saw spittle on his chin and a purple tongue snake between yellow teeth. I could see him struggling to speak. When he did, he just said one word.

"Mikey?"

The Tomorrow Tower

Then I knew he really was Frank, my brother.

*

Mom emerged from the bathroom with the aid of Andowitz. There was her vomit on his uniform, but he didn't seem to notice as he wiped my mother's chin with a towel. Mom staggered forward and held Frank in her arms. At eighteen he had been taller than Mom, but now they were the same height. Frank said nothing. He had a weird expression glued to his face. Mom set Frank at the head of the kitchen table, so he was facing the gigantic cake. We took positions next to him. Mom toasted his return. The guests drank wine with rigid unease. Frank looked too tired to care. Mom cut the cake, and the people tried to act normal, but I knew they were embarrassed. They couldn't wait to go home. Frank sat like a mannequin. One of the church ladies said that Frank was welcome on Sunday, though she looked as if she were addressing the devil. I noticed even Vanessa was drinking the vodka punch in more than liberal amounts. Frank ate some cake, a few crumbs, most of it going down his shirt. His hands were shaking. It surprised me he could hold the glass of lemonade Mom handed him, but I could see the strain on his face and knew he was doing this charade for Mom. It was Mom's return. Mom's rebirth.

Gradually, Frank's friends queued to pat him on the back or shake his lifeless hand. Then they raced for the door.

Andowitz stayed the longest. He turned to me after shaking

The Tomorrow Tower

Frank's limp hand. "I'm sorry. This was never meant to happen. If there's anything I can do ..."

He left his email address, then drove away.

We were alone with Frank.

"It's good to see you," I said to the skeleton.

Frank grabbed my arm and squeezed. His grip was so weak.

"You look -" I said. I stopped. What was I going to say? You look well? I could not lie to him. All Frank looked was alive and barely that. Weapons had ravaged his body on the cellular level I could barely understand. I had nothing to say that could say anything. Platitudes would not do.

"Is there anything I can do for you?" I asked him.

"Yes," he said. "Get me out of here, Mikey. I can't stand this. I just want to go to bed and sleep."

*

I helped Frank to the bedroom Mom had made, "like Frank would want it." Potted plants hung from handmade baskets. The furniture matched the flowery wallpaper. It was something from a romantic novel. The Frank I knew from childhood would have said something laconic and immediately pinned Marilyn Manson posters everywhere.

But this Frank was changed.

He walked unaided to the bed and tried to take off his shoes, but ended up slumped on the floor. I picked him up and helped him

41

change into the PJs Mom had got from a TV shopping mall: big, slack and flannelette.

It was then I saw the implant.

It would be practically invisible once Frank's hair grew longer.

It was a flesh-coloured slug behind Frank's left ear, a lump the size of a dime. I wondered what it was, first thinking it was some kind of cyst or boil.

Then I saw the barcode. The black lines were beside the stamp of the manufacturer.

Human Rehab Software. MODEL CITIZEN T-CD1.

*

It felt strange moving back into my old room, but that was what I did. Mom needed help to look after Frank while he was so weak. Vanessa was surprisingly understanding - but she went back to Boston to continue her PhD. She wanted me to join her as soon as possible. I promised I would only be staying a few weeks in LA. I only intended to stay until Frank was sorted out. Vanessa said Frank would never be sorted out.

Mom fed Frank like he was a baby and he didn't complain. He was too wasted away. He didn't talk much, and I hoped that was because he was still recovering after his gene therapy - not the effects of the Rehab chip. I didn't mention the chip to Mom - it would only worry her. Christ, she was afraid of the video, never mind a state-of-the-art biotechnology device plugged into Frank's frontal lobes. I kept it a secret.

I needed to know what the software did, but didn't want to send off unnecessary alarms. What was it? I tried asking Frank during his more lucid periods, but he wouldn't or couldn't say.

Frank was a void. I asked him what had happened during the war. All he said was that he didn't want to talk about the past. Like it wasn't important.

Frank gained weight and started a slow programme of exercise. I would drive him out to Venice and he'd walk up and down the beach, walk a klick a day, stop red-faced and asthmatic. He used to run *ten* miles and be fit for a game of baseball. Once Frank's moss-like beard was razored into the sink, he looked more like the young Frank. With his face fattening and colour returning, he showed some of the familiar features captured in the myriad of photos Mom had on the mantelpiece and on the 3DTV.

The shrine had its god.

But it wasn't Frank.

He looked more and more like Frank, but it was an empty shell. I couldn't get more than a few syllables out of him.

Over the weeks I spotted Rehabs in the streets - picking up litter, washing windows, gardening. Rehab implants were part of the "clean-up society" campaign - criminals, junkies, schizophrenics, ex-vets with PTS syndrome ... all converted to be good, model citizens.

They all had that stupid grin I'd seen on Frank.

Model citizens, them all.

It scared the hell out of me.

The Tomorrow Tower

*

When I came down for breakfast, Frank was eating cornflakes and watching the TV. Mom was outside, tending to her roses. I poured myself some coffee and asked Frank if he wanted a refill. He shrugged. I poured him some anyway. The TV was loud and annoying.

"Off," I said, and the TV obeyed.

Frank winced at the silence and looked at me.

"Frank, we need to talk."

Frank spooned more cereal into his mouth, avoiding my stare and ignoring me again. I felt sudden anger and grabbed his hand and lifted the spoon from his grip and tossed it into the sink. He stopped like a broken machine when lost without some menial task to perform.

"Spoon?" he said, like an infant. "Spoon?"

"Forget the spoon, Frank. What have they done to you?"

He did not reply. I could see him struggling to form a sentence. His eyes flicked from side to side as if reading a book.

"What happened to you?"

Something deep inside Frank clicked and looked lucid for a second. "Thieves," he said.

"Rehab?" I said. "They stole something from you?" I needed to get to the heart of Frank's problem and leaned forward and asked him a second time.

The Tomorrow Tower

He nodded and then started rocking in his chair. "Rehab ... thieves ... answer. War." His face was going purple with the effort. "Memory -"

It was then Mom entered and saw his distress.

"Michael, what have you done to him?" she accused and pushed me away.

I stood back as she tended to Frank. "You've given him a seizure!"

"I didn't do anything!" I said. "Rehab did something to him. Can't you see it? He wants to tell us something, but he can't. *They* won't let him."

Mom looked at me like I was mad. She had Frank under control and shooed me into the living room. I could hear Frank crying for a few minutes and Mom saying, "There. There. It's all right."

Maybe I had pushed Frank too far, but what had Rehab stolen - his memories? Had they, in their infinite wisdom, given him a 21st-century lobotomy?

I was brooding about the possibility when Mom stormed through and closed the door, so Frank couldn't hear what she had to say to me.

"Michael, tell me the truth. Did you hurt Frank?"

"Of course not!" I said, hurt by the suggestion. But Mom did not believe me and I did not know what she was thinking. I wanted to mention the Rehab software - but that would put her over the edge. She could never handle something like that. So I apologised - said it was my fault because I tried to get Frank to speak before he

The Tomorrow Tower

was ready.

"I think it would be better for all of us if you let me help Frank through this. *Alone.*" She said "alone" in a tone that would permit no arguing.

"Please, you don't understand -"

"Oh, but I do! You're jealous of Frank and -"

"That's crazy, Mom. I'm not jealous."

"- and you can't stay here any longer."

*

She threw me out – so I returned to Boston and Vanessa. Vanessa was pleased to see me. I told her how I had failed with Frank.

"You tried your best," she said. "Let time be the healer."

"But you don't understand. Rehab did something bad to him."

She knew I was holding back information and pouted petulantly. "Tell me. Don't keep it to yourself."

Reluctantly, I told her about the implant.

"Do think this biochip is affecting him or keeping him stable? I mean, I've seen them in the shops. Kids have them implanted to skip a few grades. They've got to be harmless."

"I don't know. Those biochips give me a bad feeling. Remember the fuss they made over subliminal computer advertising way back in the 1950s? That worked at a merely suggestive level of consciousness, like hypnotism. Call me old-fashioned, but I like to know what goes into my head. With those things, you never know

46

what's on them. Whatever's on Frank's chip makes him like a goddamn zombie."

"Rehab might help him adjust to normal life again. Why don't you ask Rehab yourself what they did?"

"Ask Rehab? No way. They'd probably try to implant me, too."

I started dreaming about the implant and would wake suddenly after seeing the Rehab chip grow like a mushroom, a cancerous thing that spread deep inside Frank's skull and removed his identity.

I called Andowitz. I told him about Frank.

"Man, you say a Rehab chip?"

"Yeah, he's acting like a zombie."

He was silent for a long time. "Michael ... look, why don't we meet, huh? Talk. I'm out of the service now. I'm living in San Diego, near the VA hospital."

*

Andowitz was sitting on a bench in Balboa Park, San Diego. It was a hot, cloudless day. He looked odd in civvies - aviator sunglasses, sweatshirt, jogging shorts and Space Jordans. He was watching an outdoor Shakespeare troupe performing a mime version of Hamlet. He saw me and grinned. "How was the flight?"

"Did you know your sense of taste decreases the higher you go?"

Andowtiz shook his head. "That right?"

"Unfortunately, they make the airline food compensate." I sat watching Hamlet. "Why couldn't we talk over the net?"

He spoke in whispers. "Bugs, man. There's something bad going on in the country and we've got to stop it. Before I left the service, I sneakily got my hands on some classified files you would not believe."

I was ready to believe. "Go on."

"Rehab's a division of the Defence Department. The military invented the Rehab chip as a weapon."

"A weapon? How?"

"They used to capture the enemy and fit them with so-called suicide chips. The bad guys would go back to their side, infiltrate their own HQ, then sabotage and kill everything that moved. Then the guy would blow his own brains out, destroying the evidence. Even the most loyal terrorists couldn't do a thing against the biochips."

"How come I've never heard of this?"

"The generals don't like negative publicity, that's why. Remember, the terrorists were using gene weapons, but we couldn't as part of the UN. Biochips were our way of tilting the odds, sneaking inside their underground." Andowitz looked around like an owl. "Anyway, once the war ended and we'd won, they still had the biochips. They weren't going to let billions of dollars go to waste just because peace broke out."

"Rehab -"

"Was set up to pacify subversive elements. You noticed how there's never been a race riot in five years? Coincidence? No. The politicians got their hands on civilian versions for social engineering. You think the President got where he is without vote-rigging? Rehab is more widely spread than you could possibly think."

I shivered despite the summer heat. Looking around, I saw some men jogging in circles. I wondered if they were watching us. Andowitz got up. "You jog?"

"Today I do."

We ran across the grass, deliberately avoiding the paths. There didn't seem to be anyone following, but we didn't take any chances. Andowitz didn't even break a sweat as he ran.

"I think ... and this is a guess ... that they gave Frank a biochip to go under deep cover. Special Forces were doing all kinds of experiments, turning soldiers into killing machines, free of conscience, free of pain and fatigue and humanity. I saw one or two guys go crazy in the war zone - just jump up and run at the enemy. Now I wonder if maybe they had chips." He rubbed his neck, and my eyes widened, recalling Frank's neck. "I know what you're thinking - I could have one. Well, I thought of that. I checked myself into a private clinic and had MRI scans. No trace."

They could have put that memory in his mind, I thought. They could do anything.

"Is there some way to take out a Rehab chip?"

"It's hard-wired so it would kill you to take it out," Andowitz said. "But someone smart could rewrite the code, given the technical know-how. I'm going to see a hacker tomorrow."

"Who?"

"I can't say. I'll tell you after." He checked his watch. "I've got to go. Nice seeing you, Michael."

He ran off, leaving me gasping for breath.

*

The police report claimed Andowitz was found unconscious in a subway, buried under cardboard boxes and broken bottles. He was taken to hospital in a black ambulance, but he died on the way.

Later, the coroner said there was a syringe in Andowitz's arm containing a fatal dose of jaz.

He was just another veteran who had OD'd.

*

On the 3DTV, the President looked relaxed as he spoke to the CNN reporter. "Yes, crime is a very great problem. I guarantee that in my term of office, I will reduce violent offences by another fifty percent."

"But how will you do it without increasing the budget for law enforcement?"

"By increasing the education of our young people with good, family values." He smiled at the camera. "From next month there will be free access to neurosoftware in our libraries and schools."

I switched it off.

"Turn it back on," Vanessa said.

The Tomorrow Tower

I hadn't heard her come in. "What? He's an egomaniac."

She scowled. "No, he's a great man."

"Last week you called him a jerk."

"Last week I was wrong, okay?"

I had been about to tell her about Andowitz's death, but I could tell she wouldn't be interested. I switched on the TV and left there alone. From the kitchen, I phoned Mom's number.

She picked it up. "Yes?" No hello, no warmth.

"Mom, it's me."

"Michael, I told you not to call me."

She hung up. My own mother! I tried again but couldn't get through. The line was disconnected.

That night, I waited for Vanessa to go to sleep. Slowly, I lifted the hair behind her ear and touched her neck, gently. There it was, Rehab software, just like Frank. I recoiled instantly. She woke and asked me what was wrong.

"Nothing," I lied.

I turned so she could not see my tears.

*

Garcia worked in a little diner on Sunset Boulevard, a retro place complete with Marlon Brando posters and chrome counter and jukebox. He handed me a menu and asked me what I wanted.

"I want some silicon chips."

He looked left and right, his plastic pecks flexing under his white T-shirt. "That's a tall order."

"You know someone who can cook them?"

"Maybe."

I handed him the menu. There was a stack of a thousand dollars between the pages. He slipped the money into his fake Levis. "You really want those chips cooked."

"Enough with the metaphors. When?"

"After I get off work at five. Pick me up across the street."

*

"I'm only talking to you because of Frankie," Garcia said, lighting a cigarette as the car rolled onto the highway. "Guys in the software biz don't like strangers, not with all the industrial espionage and stuff. This guy needs paying in advance."

"How much?"

"Twenty big ones."

"I already paid one grand." I'd cleared out my bank account before leaving Boston. I didn't plan to go back unless I found a way to save Vanessa from the Rehab chip. I had fifty thousand, but I acted as if twenty was too high. "I haven't got that. I'll pay ten gees."

"Fifteen, man. *Fifteen.*"

"Okay, fifteen."

Garcia directed me to a pizza place a dozen klicks out of LA. There was an anaemic youth sitting in the window, drinking a milkshake. "That's him. Call him Joe."

The Tomorrow Tower

Garcia stayed in the car, watching the highway. I sat next to Joe and ordered a pepperoni deep pan. Joe and I sat in silence until the pizza arrived. "Joe, can you help me?"

"Just eat," he said. We ate. Joe looked like a typical Microsoft workaholic. Eventually, he got up and excused himself. He hurried to the washroom.

There was a brown bag on the table. He could have been more original, but I didn't wait to criticise. I slid the bag into my jacket. Joe emerged from the washroom and walked past me as if I didn't exist. After a minute, I watched him pull away in a red pickup. I returned to the rental and looked at the goods - a spider-like object attached to an optical cable the thickness of a hair. Garcia told me the cable would fit in a Rehab chip and blank the instruction set. I dropped him off on Sunset, and he scuttled away into the crowd.

*

Night in East LA was always like an insane fireworks party. Deadly fireworks - white, red, blue tracers - arcing into the blackness. I parked the rental outside Mom's and killed the headlights. I got out and walked across the lawn. The door opened.

Mom peered through the crack. "Michael? Get off my land!"

"I have to see Frank, Mom."

She opened the door fully. Then I saw Dad's .357 pistol in her right hand. Warning signals were telling me to run, get out of there, get back in my car and hit the accelerator. I opened my mouth to say something when she aimed the gun at me and fired.

The Tomorrow Tower

The bullet hit something across the street, setting off alarms.

"Mom! Stop!"

"Shoulda gotten lessons," she mumbled. She corrected her aim - but I was moving, diving behind the trash can. Two bullets hit the can, ricocheting past my head. Running for the car, I felt a pain whip my left arm backwards. I ducked behind the car and pulled at the door. I'd locked it. Blood soaked my left arm from shoulder to elbow, and it was going numb. I fumbled my keys out and deactivated the door lock, pulled it open as the side window shattered. Another shot sounded, followed by a wet thump. There was silence.

I peered underneath the car. I could see Mom lying on the lawn and -

and her skull hung in a bloody flap.

She'd killed herself.

Blown out her brains.

I vomited.

I stood unsteadily and walked around the car. I couldn't look at the body (I had to think of it as the body, not my mother.) I could hear sirens in the distance, dopplering nearer all the time. I entered the house. "Frank? Where are you?"

There was no reply. I checked the rooms. Frank was in the kitchen eating cornflakes. Quickly, I placed Joe's device against his neck. The optical fibre found a niche in an instant, and the spider clamped over the Rehab chip. Frank started to twitch.

It was over in five seconds.

The Tomorrow Tower

"Frank? How do you feel?"

"I hate cornflakes. That's how I feel." His face broke out into a smile. "Great to see you, Mikey. I feel as if I've been in a dream. A nightmare. How'd I get here?"

"Long story," I said.

Blue-white strobe light shone through the window slats and the police squawked a warning. "You've got to get out of here, Frank. Mom's dead and they'll blame us. The police will just stick a Rehab chip back in you."

He hugged me. "Come with me."

"No. You're better off if I divert them."

He could see I was right. There was no way we'd both escape. I put my hands over my head and walked out into the bright light.

*

My trial was a farce.

Vanessa was a prosecution witness. She said I'd been acting oddly for several weeks, blaming my mother for throwing me out.

An expert witness psychologist confirmed that I had committed matricide during a psychotic episode, and ballistics experts confirmed I had pulled the trigger for the fatal shot. The defence lawyer did not object even once to the authenticity of the LAPD data.

I became so attuned to the Rehab "look" that - no matter how subtle the programming - I could tell ten out of the twelve jurors were Rehabs. The defence lawyer was one, too. Talk about rigged.

I was sentenced to Rehab.

As I led away, the court was momentarily interrupted by a red-faced clerk bursting through the doors.

"The President's been shot! The President's been shot!" The court's proceedings stopped while the judge asked for details.

Some crazy veteran had walked right up to the president and shot him in the head - one, two – *dead*.

A professional kill.

The killer had used the confusion and panic of the crowd to escape, but he had shouted some words as he fired, words that meant everything to me because it proved he was no longer a stranger.

"This is for Mikey!"

BARNEY

"I think we need an alien for Lee and Angela," Karen said, when the twins started crying for the fourth time that night.

Michael muttered something in his sleep.

Karen was tired. She had never expected motherhood to be so exhausting. Why couldn't their babies sleep at night, like normal people? But, no, they had to cry and cry all day and night, turning their parents into quivering wrecks. She got up and went to the twins' room. Their screams were like needles entering her head, jab-jab-jabbing her with a growing headache. Though the babies were cute and she loved them more than life itself, she just wished that she could have a break from their ceaseless demands. She settled them down with some breast milk, then crawled back into bed beside her husband. Michael was snoring gently. Karen nudged him in the back, and he turned over, too tired to open his eyes.

"Honey," she said, "did you hear what I said about an alien?"

"Uh-huh," he mumbled. "An alien ... but why?"

"This is the tenth time this week we've been woken up at four," she said. "The tenth time!"

The Tomorrow Tower

"There are only seven days in a week, so that technically is not acc-"

"Shut up, Mike. Shut up! You're not in the courtroom now. Open your eyes, damn you. Talk to me."

Michael looked at her. His eyes were ringed with shadows, the corneas the colour of cherries. "I'm listening, I really am."

"We need a Gabashi."

"I don't trust the Gabashi," Michael said. "I mean, what do we know about them? They say they come from some distant planet that was wiped out by a supernova? How likely is that?"

"We know they care about human beings. They're a peaceful race that loves to help younger races. They love children. I'm sure we could trust one just to look after the kids until they grow out of diapers."

"I dunno, sweetie."

He called her sweetie when he was being condescending.

"Mike, I can't become a resident if I keep falling asleep standing up. I'm dead tired every day." She saw him drifting off. She shook him awake. "Honey, you said yourself you lost the Halliman case because you couldn't think straight. That's why we need help. The Gabashi will change diapers, feed them, give them hugs, protect them."

"I dunno." He sat up, scratching his chest. "I don't like the idea of having strange aliens in the house."

Karen reached over to the bedside dresser. She opened the top drawer and pulled out her iPad. She showed him a copy of the *Time* article. "This is a great article about them."

"I can't focus this early, babe. Can't you summarise?"

"It says 'The Gabashi make perfect nannies. They are a peaceful race that want to be integrated into our society.' See? They want to help us! It's sad really. They've been alone in space for millions of years. They're lonely. We have to give them a chance, Mike. You're not going to tell me you're xenophobic?"

"The Gabashi are overgrown teddy bears, if you ask me."

"Mike! We have our careers and social lives to think about. We need rest. We're not getting any." As if to prove her point, the twins started crying again. "Besides, you will never become a partner if you don't get some sleep."

"True."

"The Gabashi have never harmed anyone or anything since they landed on Earth. Heck, they allowed us access to their mothership to prove they had no secret weapons. They wouldn't dare hurt a human being because we'd kick their butts."

"That's true," he admitted. He'd seen *Independence Day* and *Men in Black*; they would win a war with any alien critters, no matter how dangerous. "But I don't like the idea of a nanny, per se."

"The Gabashi are natural empaths, which means they can sense if Lee and Angela are upset and do something about it immediately. What kid wouldn't want an intelligent, cuddly bear looking after them?"

"I bet they charge a fortune."

"No, no, no. That's the amazing thing. The Gabashi don't need money."

"Come on, everyone needs money. Even aliens."

"They get pleasure out of being *nice*. Everyone I know who has kids is getting one."

"Oh, so you have been talking about this?"

"Sarah and Harry say the aliens take the stress off you. They'll even go shopping, clean up ... you name it."

"It'd be another mouth to feed."

"No - their digestive systems are so advanced they eat garbage and lick the dust off the furniture. We wouldn't even have to buy food for it."

"You really want this, don't you?"

"Only if you do."

She snuggled up to him, using all her feminine wiles.

"Okay," Michael said, sighing, "but let's not get too enthusiastic. I don't trust anything that does hard work for pleasure. If it does anything to hurt the kids, it's out of here, agreed?"

"Agreed."

*

They spent a couple of weeks studying the files on the Gabashi. Since all Gabashi were telepaths who shared their knowledge among their own kind, there wasn't much to choose between them except their looks. Some were cute, some really cute, and some were adorably cute. Karen and Michael finally selected a candidate out of the billion Gabashi refugees just because his name caught their attention: Barney the Bear. The aliens liked childish Earth names, which Karen found endearing. She already liked Barney before she'd met him.

Even so, Karen wanted to receive her first impression of the alien before it arrived home, in case it wasn't suitable. They left the kids with her mom and dad, then drove across the States to Nevada, where the mothership had landed at White Sands. Michael parked their Toyota Land Cruiser in the shadow of the alien ship, hovering over the desert.

Something was awe-inspiring about the Gabashi mothership. It was so huge that it blocked the sun for hundreds of miles. It was a pyramid the size of a mountain. It was also furry, like Gabashi skin. The mothership was well-guarded by Earth security forces, though the precautions were to keep alien-haters out as much as the aliens in. A US army sergeant checked their identities and the newly issued green card for Barney, then let them inside the landing zone.

Among several thousand Gabashi outside the entrance hatch, milling about in the sunlight, Barney was waiting. He was a six-foot-tall Gabashi. The alien looked like a teddy bear with soft brown fur, except for its large ears, which were creamy white and shaped like maple leaves. Its pure blue eyes blinked in the sunlight as it waddled towards them, offering its paw to Karen.

"Call me Barney," the alien said in a cartoony voice.

"Call me Karen," she said.

"Nice to meet you, Karen."

The Tomorrow Tower

Barney bowed and kissed her hand. Karen was surprised by how warm and silky its paw felt. She noted that it didn't have claws. It didn't feel as if there were any bones in it either - just a spongy material inside, like stuffing or foam. Like a real toy animal. Then Barney released her hand and smiled at Michael. "Nice to meet you, Michael."

"Thanks," Michael said, shaking hands. But he still felt uncomfortable inviting a stranger into their home. What if it was a baby-eating psycho?

"You're worried I'm dangerous," Barney said.

"I'm -"

"You've forgotten I can read your mood. Don't worry, Michael. I can assure you my race has never ever used violence. We could never hurt a thing. It's a genetic blessing. Before the supernova forced us to look for a new home, we lived in harmony with nature. The Gabashi are pacifists. All our arguments are settled through our telepathic union by discussion and reasoning. We are all part of the same mind, you see. To us, fighting would be like cutting off your nose to spite your face. That's a human expression I believe you use."

"You speak perfect English," Karen said.

"We learn fast," Barney replied. "Our scholars have studied your languages, and now we all know the same information thanks to our -"

"Telepathic link?"

"Exactly. My, Karen, you do have quite a strong intuitive sense yourself." Barney smiled, revealing a red tongue that looked like a piece of velvet. "I'd love to see your beautiful children, please. I'm so looking forward to being a part of the family. Is that your lovely car?"

"It is."

"You have great taste. It is a safe and yet comfortable model."

Michael didn't like this alien bear. It was too smooth and friendly for his liking. It wasn't natural to be so ... so polite. But he said nothing as they walked to the car. But he was worried.

*

Barney moved into the spare bedroom. Karen was soon thinking of "it" as a "he". He didn't bring any personal items because the Gabashi didn't need anything of a material nature. Karen was amazed to learn that he didn't sleep at all, for the world he had come from did not spin, so he did not need a sleep cycle. The alien was always on call for the babies, night or day. He was wonderful.

When Barney wasn't busy with the children, he would dust or cook dinner, never complaining, never tiring. He seemed to take pleasure in making other people happy.

Still, Michael kept a close eye on their new child-minder, making sure Barney treated the twins right. He installed a spy camera in the twins' bedroom without telling Karen. After a week, he was satisfied Barney wasn't going to hurt the babies; Barney was so caring and loving towards their children that it made Michael feel guilty for suspecting the worst. He wasn't a baby-eating psycho. There really was such a thing as a peaceful race. Michael removed the camera during the weekend, returning it to the security company, knowing Lee and Angela were in the best of hands while he and Karen worked.

With Barney at home, Michael could concentrate on his career. As an associate in the second-largest law firm in the Midwest, he was desperate to impress his bosses with hundred-hour weeks, more now he was free to work longer. And, when he got home, Barney would be there with a warm meal and a foot massage.

Karen was also climbing the career ladder at the hospital, a rising star in the surgical team. She was hoping to become a leading neurosurgeon. Thanks to Barney, she could also focus on her job and have a family to come home to at night and at the weekends.

Though they'd intended on having a Gabashi nanny for just a few months, there seemed no reason to send him back after the trial period. Barney was one of the family. He was like two sets of caring grandparents rolled into one body..

After two years, Michael got his junior partnership; Karen was writing articles for the top medical journals. Barney cared for the children, showed them how to play games, told them stories, and taught them how to read and write and do arithmetic.

Michael rarely got to see them for more than a few hours each day, but he was happy as long as the kids were happy. And they were happy.

Karen had a third child, Fiona, reassured that Barney could look after Fiona and it wouldn't interrupt her flourishing career. Most families were having more babies now that the pressure to be parents and workers had been reduced. The Gabashi had freed them.

Karen knew their kids would receive an excellent education because the Gabashi started teaching in the schools, and she knew they would be safe on the streets because the Gabashi started policing the streets. The Gabashi were the perfect police: they never used violence to apprehend a felon, but merely surrounded them until human officers arrived. Even if a criminal had a gun or knife, it would not harm a Gabashi, for the cute aliens had no solid organs, not even a centralised brain. If you struck a Gabashi, it was like fighting a pillow. A harmless white foam would come out if you cut a Gabashi. If you shot a Gabashi, the bullet would be absorbed by their rubbery body and heal over in minutes. The only weapon that would really hurt a Gabashi was a flamethrower, but even then that would only destroy a single body. Its companions would save the Gabashi's mind. To the Gabashi, there was no permanent death. Only love.

Michael rose in the firm, acquiring more and more important cases. He was soon bringing in over a half-million dollars a year for the firm, looking to become a senior partner. He sometimes wished he spent more time with the kids, but then he would have to give up his responsibilities in the firm. He wanted his name on the entrance plaque to the building. He could not relax until he had achieved that goal.

The Tomorrow Tower

And Karen needed to win the Beckman Award, a top award for neurosurgery. She worked harder and harder to achieve a breakthrough.

It seemed like that in no time at all, Lee and Angela were teenagers. It was then Michael, with his career fully established, realised that he hadn't spent a lot of time with them growing up. *Barney* had taken Lee to his little league games. *Barney* had shown Lee how to throw a basketball. *Barney* had told Angela about periods.

Michael talked with Karen about his concerns, but she was working hard at her research, pioneering radical brain surgery for CJD victims. She was away in Europe for most of the year, collaborating with scientists. Karen couldn't understand what he was complaining about: Barney wasn't *substituting* him, she said, but *helping* him. He wouldn't be earning a million a year without Barney's help, would he? No. He would be a lowly associate, if that. All of which was true, but it didn't make him feel better. He didn't even know what Lee and Angela and Fiona's hobbies were these days. He felt like a stranger in his own home. When he did get the kids to talk to him, all they seemed to talk about was Barney-this and Barney-that.

Michael felt as though he were the only person in the world who felt as if he'd lost something.

Then one day Karen was shocked to discover that Angela had a boyfriend called Tony, a boy she had never met. Tony was five years older than Angela. He was also a biker. Karen confronted her daughter.

The Tomorrow Tower

"I think you're too young to be seeing a boy that old," Karen said.

"*Mum*, I'm fourteen. Barney says I can do what I want as long as I play safe."

"What? Barney said that?"

"Yes, and he bought me protection, if I want to ... you know. Have sex."

Karen couldn't believe it. A fourteen-year-old girl had no business seeing a nineteen-year-old man. She confronted Barney as the alien was licking the dining room carpet clean. "Barney, have you been giving my daughter advice about sex?"

"Yes," Barney said, smiling his ingratiating smile. "I haven't offended you, have I? I thought you wanted her to know the facts of life."

"I did, but -"

"She has matured into a young woman, Karen. I was only making sure I prepared her for all circumstances."

That was reasonable, but -

"You should have told her she is too young."

"I have found that telling Angela something like that often results in her rebelling. By not making an issue out of it, she can make an informed decision about whether she has sexual intercourse with Tony or not. As she has pointed out to me, she is the same age as Juliet in Shakespeare's play. I believe it is her decision, not yours."

"Who gave you the authority to tell Angela that?"

"Why, I believe you did, Karen."

The Tomorrow Tower

The most galling this was he was right. She had. But now Barney was usurping her authority as a parent. "I want you out of here right now."

"Pardon?"

"You can't stay here any longer. Get packed and go."

"I have nothing to pack, Karen. But I will leave immediately if that is your wish?"

"Go," she said.

Barney left.

As soon as the kids found out Barney had gone, the house became a war zone. None would talk to Karen or Michael, who backed her view; they treated them as pariahs. The kids wouldn't eat the food they cooked because it wasn't as good as Barney's. They wouldn't listen to his advice. They came back from school learning things from their Gabashi teachers Karen and Michael didn't think they were ready for. There seemed to be no moral values being taught except "have fun, and the rest will take care of itself."

Angela stormed out one day to live with Tony. Then Michael caught Lee with a stash of weed which a psychology teacher had encouraged him to try. A Gabashi teacher.

Karen and Michael's family was falling apart, and both their careers were suffering as a consequence. Michael's bosses needed him to work harder, but he couldn't, not with his domestic life in tatters. Karen could not come back from Europe, not during her seminar, so it was entirely up to him. But the kids resented him, hated him, and refused to do anything he said. He employed six successive human housekeepers in an attempt to sort out the problem, but they all quit after a couple of days. The kids wanted Barney.

Barney. Barney. Barney.

It was happening all over America: the first generation of Gabashi-reared children were rebelling against their parents. Across the rest of the world, the same thing was going on. The children and teenagers were seeking instant pleasure regardless of long-term cost. The Gabashi were behind it: feeding off the good feelings the children produced by doing what made them happy, encouraging them to just enjoy themselves for the moment. The Gabashi made things so easy for the young they didn't have to think of consequences. They could just have fun. And the parents could just stand by and watch them, powerless to do anything.

There were attempts at gathering up the Gabashi and arresting them, but there were too many, and they had already won the hearts and minds of the children. For every Gabashi arrested, another merely emerged from their mothership, which was immune to Earth's weapons, being made of a material similar to Gabashi flesh.

From a legal point of view, the Gabashi had done nothing exactly illegal (except perhaps the promotion of drugs), but through their insidious use of love they had taken over the world with hardly any resistance.

The invasion had been a complete success.

And so Karen and Michael had little choice but to invite Barney back. At least that way they could work full time and contribute something to their family's life - money.

That was something, Karen and Michael supposed.

Barney returned, smiling. "Nice to see you, Karen. Nice to see you, Michael. I hope we can still be friends."

Karen and Michael said nothing.

Barney offered his palm.

Reluctantly, they shook hands.

Barney's was warm.

COUCH POTATO

I loved technology as a kid. As a kid, I was the only person in the house who could work the video. But somehow, over the years, things got a whole lot more complicated when they should have got easier. It was called progress. First, there was the internet. That was supposed to make things easier to obtain information. But what happened? Everyone got online and started producing their own personal websites, and before you knew what had happened, it was ninety-nine per cent junk, one percent useful. Then there was the explosion of multimedia and digital television, so many channels and programmes to choose from a bloke could go nuts trying to find one worth watching.

There was so much choice.

Too much.

I needed help.

The Friendly Telly was meant to solve my problems. It was one of the first intelligent machines. I'd always been uneasy about the idea of intelligent machines, but the saleswoman assured me that the only way to cope with the thousands and thousands of television channels was to have a TV that could autoselect programmes for my taste. It sounded a good idea. So I bought one.

It was a forty-inch, ultra-definition television with a machine intelligence rating of 100. That was standard for the new generation of household appliances. It was a clever machine, all right. It could talk and see and move around. It could move from room to room to save the cost of buying more than one, like a trained pet. Ideal for the couch potato.

It behaved well until recently.

It was a Friday. When I arrived home, tired and hungry, the TV greeted me with an accusatory blast of off-channel white noise.

"What's wrong with you?" I asked.

It flashed the time on the screen. I realised I was a little later than usual, but so what? I'd been out with friends. Was the TV my keeper?

"TV, what's your problem?"

A beer advert appeared on the screen.

"Yes, I've been drinking with some friends," I said, and walked to the kitchen. I didn't allow the TV in the kitchen in case it made a mess. It stopped at the door, then retreated.

Seconds later, I heard my favourite cop show coming from the living room. The TV wanted me to sit down and watch it. I ignored it. I told the microwave I was starving, and it prepared chicken in a white wine sauce. I ate in silence. Afterwards, I complimented it on the dish.

The Tomorrow Tower

The TV angrily increased the volume.

I went through. "Look, what's your problem?"

An image of a microwave.

"I don't have any feelings for the microwave!"

The TV flashed the picture on and off.

"You don't believe me?"

A blank screen.

"You're sulking now, is that it?"

Nothing.

"Put the news on."

Nothing.

"I said put the news on."

I looked for the remote control override, but the TV had hidden it.

"Put the news on!"

Nothing.

"Put the news on, *please*."

The news came on and I sat on the sofa. I was sweating and angry. The TV behaved properly the rest of the night, but then when I wanted to go to bed.

It followed me into the bedroom without permission.

"Hey! TV, switch off."

It ignored me.

I could not believe it.

It wouldn't switch itself off.

The Tomorrow Tower

*

"What are the symptoms?"

"Jealousy, sulkiness, anger - it's worse than my ex."

"It sounds like Turing Syndrome." The repairman confirmed my worst doubts, that my TV was a few components short of a calculator.

"Is it serious?"

"I'd have to ask it a few questions to answer that. How long have you had the TV?"

"Three years."

"And how long has it behaved negatively?"

"A couple of weeks."

"Hmmm - yes, it's Turing Syndrome. It's a problem we get with machines that spend too much time with a particular person. The software that recognises you - the user - becomes so familiar that it needs you to function. It expects you. It wants you. Essentially, it's machine love. It's a fairly rare complaint, I'm glad to say. You must spend a lot of time watching TV?"

"Yeah, I'm a couch potato, but what can you do?"

"They don't call me a TV repairman for nothing."

*

Friendly Telly was waiting for us when we entered my flat. It sprung into life, splitting the screen into sixteen of my favourite channels, ready to obey instructions like a good little TV.

The Tomorrow Tower

I didn't believe it for a minute.

I stayed at the door as the repairman knelt down and inspected the TV's control panel. "TV, show Channel 9," he said.

Channel 9 came on.

"Sports."

Sports.

"Something with Burt Reynolds."

Smokey and the Bandit II.

"Something good with Burt Reynolds."

The screen went blank.

"See?" he said. "It works."

"Try it with something harder," I said.

"TV, what's the situation in Uganda?"

The CNN World Report War in Uganda Special.

The repairman shook his head. "It looks okay to me."

"It doesn't normally listen. I think it's just doing it for your benefit."

"I see," said the repairman. "Perhaps the audio chips are faulty?"

He ran a diagnostic and found nothing wrong. "Maybe its voice recognition is faulty. Ask it something."

"What?"

"For a programme you like."

"Um ... local news."

Local news.

"It's obeying because you're here," I said.

The Tomorrow Tower

I could tell the repairman was sceptical, but he said that he would take it away for a full test.

"Do it," I said.

*

"There's an urgent message," said the answering machine.

"Show me it."

It was the repairman. He looked embarrassed. "Ah, Mr Stansbrook, there's a problem with your TV. You must call me as soon as possible. Thank you."

"Call him back."

He was pleased to see me. "I must apologise in advance, Mr Stansbrook, but it's not my fault."

"What's not your fault?"

"The accident."

I felt sick. "Accident?"

"With the TV."

"You've damaged my TV?"

He nodded. "You'll be fully compensated for the price of a replacement, but that's not what concerns me. You see, we carry out a test by uploading the memory into our Diagnostician and treating the software. It's a bit like going to a psychiatrist. That's when the feedback loop occurred."

"I don't understand."

"A high voltage was sent into the television and blew the whole motherboard. Your TV considered this a deliberate attack and fought back."

"Hang on, we're talking about a machine, right? How can a machine fight back? What does it do? Send some explicit binary code down the line?"

"The software entered our artificial intelligence and then disappeared down the phone lines. I'm afraid the accident may have given your machine the idea that you wanted to kill it, so I'm warning you to be careful."

"You're saying my TV wants revenge?"

"Yes."

"Is it dangerous?"

"Hard to say. You might want to contact the police, though, just to be on the safe side."

*

I met Sandy for lunch. I told her about my TV. Sandy sipped a cappuccino and tried to absorb the repairman's warning with a seriousness that she couldn't maintain. "Let me get this straight. Your TV wants to kill you?"

"Maybe."

She laughed at the absurdity and caused half a dozen people to turn and look at me. I shrunk down to the size of an amoeba.

"This is serious, Sandy. I've been to the police."

"You haven't?"

The Tomorrow Tower

"I have. The police say there's nothing to worry about, but I'm worried."

"You actually told the police that your telly is out there on the loose with a vendetta?"

"The repairman suggested I contact them."

"He must be as crazy as you."

"It's not funny."

"Of course not. It happens all the time. Why only the other day the dishwasher spun a plate at me like a ninja because it doesn't like dried-on stains."

"Forget I said anything."

"My lips are shut." She mocked a zipping gesture. "See?"

*

But I couldn't forget.

It started with little things that could have been coincidental if I didn't know better. Such as the answering machine saying someone was calling, but then the caller left no message. It happened each night for a week - until I contacted the telephone company. I told them that I was getting crank calls. They took that very seriously. Their records showed that the calls had been made from different numbers. Each connected to a different home computer where there had been unauthorised access. My television was moving around the town. The next time it happened, they were on the location in seconds and shut down the system, hoping to trap it. But they were too slow.

A police officer came to my home. Detective Johanne McKlusky looked like the sort of man who would be more at home living in a subway than policing the "superhighways of crime" - his favourite phrase. He had a goatee beard and greasy hair that ran down his shoulders and smelled of mildew. I felt like I'd invited the gutter inside my apartment. "In our experience rogue, AIs have individual mental problems. This one believes it is in love with you."

"I understand all that, but what's actually been done to find my TV?"

"With the phone company's help, we are tracing its route through the internet. It's got to appear in one of our servers sometime, and that's when we'll nab the critter with the department's computer. It shouldn't take long. A matter of nanoseconds once your TV makes its next move."

"Is it dangerous?" I asked, again. Nobody had given me an answer.

"There was a case of a jealous car that crashed into a wall when it found out its owner was going to buy a new car. What a scrape that was ... but don't worry about it. Nothing's going to happen like that ... I don't think. Since the TV loves you, it's unlikely to harm you. It's more likely to harm your loved ones."

"Gee - thanks for the comforting words."

"Do you drive?"

"Yes."

"Does it have a computer brain?"

The Tomorrow Tower

"Yes."

"Keep it off the road until things are sorted out. We should have a result in a day."

I thanked him and got him to leave.

I sat down on the couch.

Then the answering machine said, "Hello, again."

Then nothing more.

It had to be the TV. It probably knew the detective had just left.

My TV was doing its best to psych me out.

And it was succeeding.

*

Sunday morning. Sandy entered my apartment and found me hunched over a bowl of cereal, spooning soggy wheat flakes into my mouth.

"You look terrible," she complimented.

"Thanks."

"This place is a bomb site. It tried to call ... but I see you've pulled the phone off the wall and thrown it across the room."

"I had a disagreement with it."

"Is the TV still calling?"

"Not any longer now that I've pulled the phone off the wall and thrown it across the room."

"That wasn't very mature of you."

"Tell the TV."

The Tomorrow Tower

Sandy sat and pushed the bowl away from me. "We need to talk."

"We do?"

"About our relationship."

"Ah. Our relationship."

"Your TV is coming between us and ... and I don't know what to think. It's all you talk about. What did you do to make the TV so obsessed?"

"Me? I didn't do anything."

"Are you sure?"

"Sandy, don't look at me like I'm sleeping with your best friend. Do you think I encouraged my TV to fall in love with me?"

"You just said *my* TV and not *the* TV. Doesn't that say something?"

"Sigmund Freud's turning in his grave, Sandy."

"You're avoiding the question."

"What question?"

There were tears in her eyes.

"Did you ... you know ... encourage it?"

"What? I don't believe I'm hearing this. It's a television. How the hell could I encourage it? Buy a new remote control? Put a goldfish bowl on its top? Press its buttons?"

"You pressed its buttons?"

"Uh, of course, I ... but that doesn't mean anything ... the contrast was ... and I ... I can't believe you are making me feel guilty! It was just an ordinary TV and it's gone insane. Simple as that.

81

The Tomorrow Tower

Okay?"

"No. No, it's not okay!"

She stormed out before I could say a word in defence.

*

I was certain I was being followed. I was standing on the platform waiting for the tube, dressed in a thick overcoat to fight off the cold, my breath frosting in the air, when that feeling occurred and I knew there was someone watching.

I looked at the commuters. They were a stern-faced bunch, collected in groups of threes and fours. The nearest clique was chatting about work. They were not watching me.

A security camera twitched in my peripheral vision. When I turned to look at it, it started to move away like I had caught it in the act of voyeurism. Was my TV keeping a close eye?

The crowded morning tube arrived. I boarded it. I felt sure the cameras were watching me. That paranoid suspicion followed me as I got to my station and walked the streets to the office. On a whim, I stopped at a café and made a call to Sandy. Her face appeared on my screen.

"Bob, it's only eight in the morning," she said.

"Sorry, but I had to see you ... you know ... after yesterday."

"I need to take a shower, Bob."

"Right. Yeah. Can I see you after work?

"What for?"

The Tomorrow Tower

"To show you there's never ever been anything between me and the TV. I hate the stupid thing. We can talk about our relationship and stuff."

"I guess I was kind of silly."

"How about a romantic meal for two in a plush restaurant?"

"Sounds wonderful ... who's paying?"

"Very amusing. Six o'clock?"

She pouted her lips and threw a kiss. Things were looking better.

*

The morning went smoothly, and I had time to make reservations at Le Grande, one of those swanky French places with an arty menu with no prices because they alter each week. After a light lunch of coffee and office talk, I returned to find Maurice Winthorpe Junior, the son of the director, in my office, playing with the filing cabinet. He liked to play with the filing cabinet. It was the one thing he could touch and not break. He stopped when he saw me and grinned.

"A woman called, wanting to know if you meant what you said this morning."

"Sandy?"

Maurice shook his head. "Her name was Theresa."

"Never heard of her. What was her second name?"

"Vaughan, Voig? Something like that. Remember now?"

Theresa Vaughan.

The Tomorrow Tower

Initials: TV.

My throat went dry. The TV had listened to my phone call to Sandy. And I had said that I hated it.

I ordered my phone to locate Sandy, but its limited intelligence failed. "Sandy is not located near a phone."

That was impossible. Sandy always wore a phone link earring when she went out of her house. There was no way she'd forget it. Everyone wore a phone of some sort as a habit, part of the daily wardrobe.

"Maurice, what did Theresa look like?"

"Dark hair, blue eyes. Like that girl in that commercial for Sun soap. You know the one?"

Not like the girl in the Sun soap commercial, but the girl in the Sun soap commercial. My TV knew I liked that ad.

*

"Sit down and relax," Detective McKlusky told me.

"How can I relax when Sandy's missing?"

"There's not much we can do until the TV contacts you."

"My TV has got a lot smarter since it escaped. It held a conversation with a human and used a woman's image. I thought a machine intelligence of a hundred was equivalent to a cat or dog. How is this happening?"

"We suspect your TV has accessed a far greater MI and that's why it has been difficult to trace."

The Tomorrow Tower

"Has it kidnapped Sandy?"

"Probably. The behaviour of an MI with Turing Syndrome is too hard to predict with any certainty. It passed the Turing Test with Maurice Winthorpe ... where human speech was previously not in its capacity ... so its linguistic level must have been increased by a merger with a 500+ MI."

"All this is very interesting, but there's got to be something you can do NOW!"

"If your TV has any sense, it will be off the net and in some portable unit. If that's the case, there is no way our resources can confine the perpetrator. We are doing everything in our power. I'm sorry if that isn't the answer you want to hear."

"Well, that's great. So, when Sandy's body is found face down in the Thames, I can thank you for it?"

"There are a couple of questions that need answering, sir. Did you lead the TV to believe that you had feelings for it?"

"What? Did I hear you right?"

"Please, we need to know the answer."

"No."

"Did you push any of its buttons?"

Luckily for him, he dodged my fist.

"They are just questions, sir. We don't mean to offend."

"The door is that way."

"We'll get back to you with any information uncovered in our inquiries."

The Tomorrow Tower

*

I had to get out of the apartment and go somewhere miles from the stares of television screens. Hyde Park – with its muggers and rapists and hard-selling ice-cream pedlars – would be better than worrying about Sandy.

In my company car, I switched on the automatic driver and said, "Hyde Park."

The car left the car park, avoiding the worst of the traffic by cutting through side streets. I looked at the phone connection, which I had taken off as the detective suggested. The TV could kill me if I joined it to the autopilot. I could not find the TV. But the TV could find me. I plugged the phone in.

The car jerked like it had been given an injection of rocket fuel. My neck was given a painful jolt. The car accelerated through the slow-moving lanes, building up enough speed so that when it crashed, the safety bags and brakes would not save me. The TV wanted to kill me.

"Slow down! I want to talk!"

The car left the motorway without slowing, bumping over the curb and steering towards the side of a house.

"Let's talk it over! I'm ready to listen!"

Two seconds from impact, there was only one thing to try. "I love you!"

It turned at the last moment, timing it so perfectly that paint marks were left on the brick before it rejoined the road. Then it made a U-turn into heavy traffic, spinning in a tight 180 that pushed by arms against the window before it settled on a course towards the docks.

The TV had chosen a clichéd place to keep a kidnap victim, stolen from a thousand thrillers that it had seen in the three years it had been part of my life. A derelict warehouse.

The car stopped inside the entrance and the doors unlocked. I stepped out, brushed myself down and checked no limbs were missing.

I could see Sandy. She was tied to a chair with ropes. Her hair was mussed, but she was alive. It was another cliché, but the TV considered it real life.

And there it was in its new body: sleek metal, perfect curves and a chrome finish. It was a TV with mechanical arms and legs. It was Robowife.

"You love me?" the TV said.

I wanted to laugh at its attempt at being human, but it was dangerously close to Sandy. Also, its voice was imploring and needful and I did feel a little sympathy for it.

"Let her go and we can discuss this."

"You had that man try to kill me!"

"The repairman? It was a mistake."

"Lies. You wanted me out of the way so you could live with her."

The TV advanced on Sandy, fingertip drills starting to whir.

It was going to kill Sandy.

The Tomorrow Tower

Unless I stopped it.

"Don't hurt her. I'm the one that did you wrong."

The TV stopped. Undecided.

"If we can't be together in life, perhaps in death?"

"Be rational. You have everything to live for. You're intelligent and beautiful."

"I am?"

"Sure. I mean, for example, take that car. It's very clever how you used it to bring me here. How did you do that?"

"It's got a feeble brain. Stupid. All it thinks about is mileage and traffic flow and -"

The TV was silenced when the car struck. It flipped into the air, bouncing on the car's roof and boot before striking the ground. The car reversed. There was a painful crack as TV's screen shattered and parts burst on fire.

I stared at the smouldering wreckage.

It was dead.

The car stopped, satisfied that the insult had been paid for in full.

I untied Sandy, who was shaken but okay. The car flashed its headlights and opened the door for us.

"Thanks, car."

The car horn sounded.

Sandy looked at me in wonder.

"Do you have that effect on all machines?"

"Only if you press the right buttons."

TUMBLEWEED

Woody's past surrounded him whenever he walked through the hangar, like stepping into a museum. Rows of video games from his youth: flashing screens, gyrating booths and loud FX.

He had mounted as trophies early virtual reality headsets and gloves that had all the life of a piece of wood. Those games were awful with their poor graphics and slow updates … but he loved them. Gave you a headache, staring at those so-called 3D views. He played them occasionally just to have a laugh.

In those days, computers had numbers for names and the most important consideration was how many megahertz does it do? He wasn't sure what prefix they were using now because it was a hertz of a lot more. Bad puns were a favourite of his Artificial Intelligence, Sandy, and he'd picked up the habit from her.

"There's a call from Paul Scheiner," Sandy said. "Do you want to take it?"

"No. I'll call him back."

"He says it's urgent."

"I'll call him back."

The Tomorrow Tower

He did not want to face the tech. Scheiner was too nervous about the program they were running, and nervousness was infectious. Instead, he walked to his favourite antique.

Woody had picked the cooler up at a garbage site. He found it buried under a tonne of dappled newspapers and decaying biodegradables - still in a condition that he considered good enough to repair. He had spent a week fixing it up right, putting back the insides like they were originally - using an old manual he had bought for his collection as a rough guide.

Now it hummed with electricity as the centrepiece of his show, the red and white Coke logo same as on the old vids he loved. He kept the coke machine well stocked with the new cans that needed no refrigerator but looked good coming out of the hatchway. He liked to put cents in the machine and press the button. Hear the clunk and thud. See the can pop out.

Nostalgia. He sometimes thought nostalgia was a disease caught by people in their twenties for the things they liked as kids (or hated, but thought they liked) or a mental problem. But - hey - so what if it were? What makes you happy, right?

He pulled the ring pull - tzzzz - and gulped caffeine.

"Will Tumbleweed be ready for tomorrow?" he asked Sandy.

"There are no problems so far. Their security is a joke."

He wondered where Sandy had heard that informality. A joke. Everything was a joke. He was about to ask when it happened again, the shift of his body into another time.

He was no longer in the hangar nursing a coke - but holding a

90

joystick and falling, the sky and the ground twisting into view under a broken cockpit.

"Punch out!"

The words haunted Woody. He remembered the cry of static and the sound of the flight commander ordering him to eject before it was too late. But his mind raced incoherently thanks to the army-issued amphetamines that were supposed to improve his reactions.

"I'm nothing but a tumbleweed!"

He felt for the eject - there! - fought against the tide of g-force, pressed the button ready for the kick into the air.

And nothing.

Then the realisation that it wasn't working because the circuits, everything, had been blown by the impact.

So much blood in the shattered cockpit he saw nothing. *I'm a tumbleweed. Tumbleweed. Can't punch out! I can't!*

And then he was lying on the floor of the hangar with the roof spinning above him and the whining in his ears receding. He could taste blood here and in the memory. He discovered he had bitten his tongue.

He heard something coming from the entrance to the hangar.

It was the metal grille lifting. He felt panic. Nobody was supposed to know he was here!

He saw a shadow at the entrance, the figure stocky and towering compared to his slight frame.

He saw a gun.

The intruder said coldly and tonelessly: "Hello. I've been sent to

The Tomorrow Tower

kill you."

*

Someone was sitting heavily on Buchannon's stomach, holding down his arms, staring at him through the slits of a ski mask.

It was all a dream. That was Buchannon's first thought, lying there bathed in sweat, waking from a nightmare that was just beginning to get much, much worse.

"Don't move a muscle," muttered Ski Mask. Buchannon knew he was dead, right then, if he didn't fight. He reflexively bucked his hips to throw the stranger off, but it was expected. There was no strength in him to match the downward pressure and bulk of the man. Ski Mask struck a nerve centre and Buchannon felt pain kick behind his eyes. "Got ourselves a hero?"

He'd remember Ski Mask: the pin-prick, drugged eyes, the flecks of black in green irises; the smell of expensive cologne, and the stark musk of his breath. No ordinary house-breaker.

Buchannon could feel his gun under the pillow beneath his head, so close and yet unreachable. It made him as mad as hell. Mad that this situation could have happened. Mad that he hadn't already killed this SOB with a bullet in the head. But it was too late.

The second intruder switched on the bed lamp.

"Pleasant dreams, Buchannon?"

He knew the voice. Silkily erotic, so feminine it was hard to hate its owner, but he did. "Melanie Winters?"

The Tomorrow Tower

"It's been a long time," she said.

Ski Mask let Buchannon turn his head to see Melanie as she lit a cigarette and blew smoke in his face. She was wearing a black unisex suit - ideal for sneaking into bedrooms in the small hours. Buchannon wondered who made the clothes for such covert operations. They had probably liked Catwoman's outfit. Melanie looked good in the sleek material. Dark hair, cut short. Cheekbones a model would die for. Body moving with cat-like grace. And in her right hand was a hypodermic needle filled with a translucent liquid that he didn't like the look of at all.

She held it up to the light, so he could see it, and squeezed out any air bubbles. "Wouldn't want you to die of a heart attack, would we?"

With painful slowness, she brought the needle to bear on his arm and pushed the point through his skin. Ski Mask's eyes flitted briefly to the spot and Buchannon used this moment to attempt a second escape ... and found himself gasping and aching from sternum to neck, unable to move as Melanie punctured his arm successfully and released the fluid.

"There! Not so bad, was it?" she said. There was a hint of menace in her tone. "Will you behave now while we talk?"

He nodded. There wasn't much else he could do.

Ski Mask rolled off Buchannon and stepped away. It was a fatal mistake. The way Buchannon figured it, he had nothing to lose now. His hand slipped under the pillow, grabbed the gun, brought it out fast and aimed. He aimed at Ski Mask and fired once, twice, and saw the bullets hit home, striking the man in the heart and his face and throwing him backwards. No blood, but maybe that was because the room was dark. He turned to do the job on Melanie, but she was moving towards him at an angle that he simply couldn't get his gun to before she struck, sending the weapon across the room and taking apart the ceiling with a third blast. The impact broke half of his fingers, but adrenaline kept the pain at bay. He went for her eyes with pointed fingers. She hit him with a flat palm, knocking the wind from him. He lay back, gasping for air.

"Your reaction time is way down, Buchannon," she said, pulling a stun gun from a pocket. "But I'm glad to see you still sleep with your weapon ready."

Buchannon said nothing. *At least* he'd got Ski Mask.

But then there was a movement from the corpse, which sat up and said groggily, "Ohhh, man, what calibre was that?"

"Thirty-eight," Melanie said.

Ski Mask stood. "He's unstable, way he went for his gun like that." Ski Mask pulled off the mask to rub his jaw, which was bruised but intact. Buchannon saw the indented mask where the bullet had hit the surface, just below the nose, and was shock-absorbed by the plating. No doubt he had body armour to match. Buchannon didn't recognise the face, but he knew the type. Special forces. Like Melanie.

"What did you inject me with? It sure wasn't a tranquilliser!"

Melanie nodded. "It was a lethal neural toxin."

She needed three blasts of the stun gun to save herself from

The Tomorrow Tower

Buchannon's rage. When Buchannon lay limp and definitely under control, she smiled. "We bagged ourselves a real prize this time."

*

There had been a time he loved Melanie. He had been based in Tel Aviv as part of the rapid response 103rd Marines and she was an officer for Weapons and Tactics. They met at a bar near the airbase that the Saudis reluctantly tolerated in exchange for Western aid. She approached him and asked if he wanted a drink. She was very direct.

"Only if you tell me your name," Buchannon said, attempting to sound cool.

"Lieutenant Melanie Winters ... but while we're off duty, I'm ordinary Melanie. You look like you need company."

"You're right, Melanie. I've had a hard day."

"Tell me about it," she said, and meant it.

*

The shattered Stealth fighter burned like charcoal. It had crashed nose-first into the asphalt and left a black scar along the ground where it must have hopped and skipped, leaving plastic and metal fragments in its wake.

Curious children picked at the debris, but they were scared away by Buchannon running towards the crashed plane.

The smoke stung Buchannon's eyes as he looked for the

remains of the pilot. Nobody could survive that crash. He could hear sirens over the flames. He had a couple of minutes to check for the body and then he'd have to save his own skin by getting back to the team and then the landing zone.

Most of the plane's fuselage and the right wing billowed with dense smoke and the left wing was dug in the ground like a shark's fin. He spotted the pilot ejection seat five, six metres behind the main bulk. Blood on the ground. The parachute had not opened because the seat ejected too low to the ground. Unlucky. Nevertheless, he approached. He found a seriously burned man in the seat and immediately thought the man was dead. His face was charred and his flight suit was covered inh blood. Here was not the place to see if the pilot was dead, so he unbuckled the body and carried him through the wreckage, away from the approaching enemy. He settled in an alleyway and looked for vital signs.

There was a weak pulse, and the man opened his eyes.

"Tumbleweed," he said, and passed out.

*

"Who was the kid you rescued?"

He finished another beer, feeling groggy. But the perky captain kept him talking. "I think of him as the Woodsman because it was on the side of his plane."

"Edward Woody?"

"You heard of him?"

The Tomorrow Tower

"Best pilot the Gulf has seen ... you say he's badly burned?"

"Uh-huh. I don't think he's going to make it, not with half the hospitals bombed to bits."

"I'll do something," she said. Melanie went to the wall phone and returned a minute later.

"I've got him transferred to HQ."

So, he knew she was well connected.

She could afford to buy him another beer.

*

"We need you to do another mission."

"And this is how you ask?" Buchannon said. He was strapped to a leather chair, facing a white wall, aware that Melanie was behind him with maybe half a dozen people he hadn't seen and would no doubt never see. Far as he could tell, they were not military. Ex-army people had a certain way of talking that he didn't catch from these men. That meant they were rich, if they could afford to get out of being drafted.

"We need you to find a man."

"You could have asked me. What's with this neurotoxin?"

"A guarantee. There are only a few clinics in the world that do the treatment and only our influence and money will save you. You do us a favour and we will remove the virus."

He swore.

The Tomorrow Tower

Melanie laughed. She knew he feared a slow death. His mother had contracted a bio-engineered virus back in 2036 and he had seen her waste away to a husk, dying in a crowded ward surrounded by strangers. Melanie had chosen the threat perfectly.

"You get cured in exchange for helping us."

"Who's the 'us'?"

She ignored him.

The white wall flickered and changed to old military personnel images. A head shot of a face he'd last seen ten years ago. The Woodsman.

"Edward Woody. Was a friend of yours?"

He nodded.

"Went AWOL from the veterans' hospital psych ward."

This he did not know. He'd presumed the Woodsman was dead. A lot of his friends were. "He had mental problems?"

"A drug-related psychosis that has got worse despite professional aid. He thinks everyone is out to kill him."

"Why?"

"He's insane, Buchannon. You know the problems yourself - living in cheap motel rooms with your memories eating your sanity. He killed a doctor and two security men in his escape."

Silence.

Another voice. Male, crisp, New England accent. "Edward Woody disappeared for two months. Then, on the Fourth of July, the Eastern SUBNET was hit by a military AI using cracking software called Tumbleweed. The details don't concern you, but it has stolen vital data from many important projects that I and my partners need. The state of economic balance is in jeopardy."

"Shame," Buchannon said.

"We believe you know the significance of the term 'tumbleweed' to Edward Woody."

"Tumbleweed means losing complete control over an aircraft."

"In this case, it meant losing control of our data. We need the data back, and we want you to stop him from using Tumbleweed again."

"You mean ... kill him?"

"If that is what it takes."

"Why me?"

"Because you are someone he trusts."

*

He could never forget the war because there were things - little things - always present that reminded him of it. He could be walking down a street and hear a baby crying and he'd be back there, shooting at the windows of a stucco-walled house, knowing that children were in the same room as the enemy, knowing that the enemy was a mother with a rifle that had killed his buddy with a head shot two seconds before.

Buchannon was on the street again, clean-shaven and dressed in a suit he could never have afforded, with a pocket full of money and fake ID supplied by the never generous Melanie. He was aware of the number of eyes watching him, some human, some electronic. Melanie was keeping close tabs on him, and that made him careful. He did not know how to proceed.

There was one thing he knew: Melanie would not keep her word. She planned to kill him after his job was done. So, he had few options. He could sit down and die, attempt suicidal revenge, or, the third option, find the Woodsman.

He was in the Woodsman's birthplace, a small town called Hindley in New England. The contrast between the twentieth and twenty-first centuries created a feeling of homeliness. There were none of the harsh ferrocrete monoliths that so cluttered New York. The preferred architecture here was aesthetically pleasing, low-level units, red-bricked, flora abundant. He walked towards his destination, an Edwardian-style house complete with acres of lawn and oak trees.

When he reached the door, he stopped and adjusted his tie. He was choking. The hidden security camera contacted the owner and identified Major Alan H. Buchannon. The door opened.

"Please come in, sir," uttered the speaker, "the master is in the drawing room. That is the second on your right."

He nodded, though it wasn't necessary for the Artificial Intelligence. The drawing room smelled musty. It was also gloomy. The drapes were half-closed. A man in his early hundreds sat reading a webmag and only looked up when Buchannon politely coughed.

"You're the one that rescued my son when his plane crashed." It was not a question. Buchannon waited for more, aware that there was deep intelligence in the blue eyes of Ronald Woody. "What brings you here?"

"Some vets are having a reunion, going to share the good times. I was wondering -"

"Stop. I'm afraid you've come a long way for nothing. He's not here."

Buchannon sensed the weariness and caution in Ronald Woody. His answer was too sharp. Prepared.

"I've heard he got into trouble ... and I thought ... I thought I could help. I believe in the Chinese tradition of once you save a life, you have to take responsibility for their soul forever. I want to help."

"There's something you're not telling me."

He knows.

"What?"

"You're troubled, like Edward. You have it in your eyes. That lost look. My father had that look. Do you really want to help Edward?"

"Yes." He tasted the sour deceit on his tongue.

"The war ruined his life, you know, and the thing I can't understand is that he actually volunteered. There was no need. We have money and he could have gone to college, but he was a fool."

"I don't think that."

"A decade has gone, Major, and in that time, what has winning the war achieved? Has poverty vanished? Has hatred gone? No. It was a waste. Such a waste."

"Losing would have been worse."

The Tomorrow Tower

"Perhaps."

"The past stains us all, sir. Please let me help your son. Has he contacted you?"

"What can you do for him?"

Kill him? Is that what you can do?

"I don't know. Yet."

Ronald Woody shrugged. "I don't know where he is. I'm sorry."

"So am I."

"Time is not a great healer. It's the opposite. The more time that passes creates a chasm between people that gets larger and larger until there's a Grand Canyon of a difference and it's too late. Don't you think?"

*

Buchannon left Hindley on the Amtrak shuttle with a ticket booked for Detroit, knowing he would have to think fast and act faster. He bought clothes from the onboard tailor and retreated to a lavatory. There, he stripped and checked himself in the mirror for blemishes that could possibly signify the placing of a tracer or transmitter. He found one in his hair that they obviously meant him to find. It was easy to feel with probing fingertips, and another on his back beneath his epidermis that wasn't. He steeled himself and removed it with a razor, and put it in his wallet for the moment. He hoped that was it.

The mirror showed a man he barely recognised. Hollow eyes, in a tired face. Muscles that had lost their strength during his period of

The Tomorrow Tower

enforced civility.

*

He remembered the day the war ended as the worst day of his life. June 11th, 2031.

The 103rd had taken control of an underground complex and were clearing bodies and taking prisoners. He had been assigned to protect Lieutenant Winters while she took control of the enemy's equipment. He heard the sounds come from a storage room.

"Possible threat, Lieutenant."

She nodded, and they proceeded to either side and raised rifles. He kicked the door in and there was the kick of gunfire, and Buchannon noted the position and distance of the enemy soldier. He rolled into the room and located the target, a private left by his commanders to hold the base. Buchannon killed him. It was over in seconds. There were more people in the room, children and old people sheltering from the bombs.

"It's okay, Lieu -"

He would remember the stutter of Melanie's gun and the brief screams of the people as they fell, bloodied and lifeless.

"What did you do that for?"

"I saw a gun," she said.

He knelt amongst the bodies and searched for some proof to keep his belief in his lover, some sign that these people were not innocent and she had been right.

The Tomorrow Tower

He never found the weapon.

The worst day of his life.

*

He dressed in the new clothes after checking them. You could never be too careful. He was as sure as he could be that he was clean of bugs. He slipped out of the toilet and debarked at the next stop.

He bounced around town, giving false trails to Melanie's employer, putting the bug on a man in the airport and buying a seat on every flight that hour. Let Melanie follow that. Then he disappeared.

*

Buchannon wiped a day's dust from his hands and looked out at the Grand Canyon through binoculars, hoping to see something that registered as a calling card. Ronald Woody was a sly devil, he mused, probably knew that he was being watched. He could have slipped into the location like a pro without being noticed. Buchannon put away the binoculars and returned to his car, driving to the nearest hotel for a meal and a place to rest.

He asked the clerk if there were many hotels around and was informed that most had closed down in the recession and this was the last frontier, as far as sightseers were concerned. He ate and slept. He woke at six. The sun did not rise until an hour later. His mind had been at work during his sleep, and he had an idea why the

The Tomorrow Tower

Woodsman had contacted his father from the Grand Canyon.

He'd visited the burned pilot in the veteran's hospital. The Woodsman had become a sort of mascot for the 103rd and, after surgery, he looked a hundred times better than when he dragged him from the wreckage.

"Thanks for getting me out, Buck."

"Sure. Any young nurses taking care of you?"

Woody laughed. "One or two."

"Going easy on them, eh?"

"You know why I learned to fly? I met a girl when I was fourteen. Sandy, her name. During a vacation at the Grand Canyon, we stayed at the Holiday Inn. We fancied each other like crazy, but she would not go further than a kiss. Can you believe that? When I asked her why, she told me that she wanted to marry a fighter pilot, a Top Gun, and anything less would not do. That's why I decided to become a pilot."

"Better reason than most. What happened to Sandy?"

Woody shrugged. "Who knows? We didn't even trade email addresses."

"She's probably still waiting for a war hero like you!"

Buchannon drove on to the location of the Holiday Inn and inquired at the desk for the logbook. He showed his fake police ID and got into the records. In general, businessmen paid by credit cards and one reference stood out for a cash payment dated one day after the Woodsman escaped. There were other guests that day, but intuition was enough for Buchannon.

The Tomorrow Tower

The guest had used the phone twice, and the numbers and length of calls were listed. The first call was to Ronald Woody; the second, unknown.

Information told him that the number was out of service, but he got the address printed and returned to his car. The number had gone out of service a week *after* the Woodsman used it.

*

Apartment 6B was in the name of Paul Scheiner. The rent had been paid three months ahead, so the landlord presumed it was occupied, which was wrong. Detective Doherty (as Buchannon introduced himself) learned that no one had seen anyone go near 6B for some time, but that wasn't exactly unusual with the people in this part of the city. People kept pretty much to themselves.

Buchannon let himself into the apartment and could smell it had been abandoned in a hurry because there was a stuffiness to the room. The furniture remained. It looked like the shelves, tables and drawers had been emptied rapidly into bags and carried outside. Scheiner had left no deliberate trails. Buchannon searched the rooms, finding spoiled food in the kitchen and extra blankets and pillows on a couch - Woody had been here. He left the room as he found it and located a public comlink. There he called information requesting any travel tickets bought by P. Scheiner in the last month. None. This he expected because Scheiner wasn't stupid. Scheiner was a tech, so any clues would be of a physical nature, not a virtual

The Tomorrow Tower

nature.

He took a risk of losing the trail completely. He called Scheiner's only living relative, his sister who lived nearby - after installing a tap on her line that would record her messages.

"Hello, is Paul there yet?"

"Paul?" She sounded puzzled.

"He said he'd be at yours today."

"Who are you?"

She was suspicious.

"I'm the Woodsman."

She hung up, which meant she had seen the real Woody. Buchannon waited a few minutes and then accessed the net. Miss Scheiner had made a call. The number was a fake connection, but Buchannon watched the video. She spoke to Scheiner, worriedly, and he told her to be careful to not call again. He'd call her. Buchannon took the video to a film booth and studied the images. The thing with 3D was that there was always something in the picture if you looked at the right angle. He hoped. Behind Scheiner, there was a worktop. By enhancing the image, Buchannon could see the top of a box of pizza. He peered at the image and smiled.

*

It was a ghost town, way out in the desert. Buchannon visited the pizza place, a family concern since the 1970s, according to the drawling Pop behind the counter. A little piece of history. He described Scheiner and got a positive response because the guy was good on faces. Scheiner had been in just yesterday.

And that was it.

This was the place that the Woodsman would choose to hide. A dark spot in the past.

He went to the jack station, recharged his car, and then bought a local map. One glance and the place leapt at him, saying X marks the spot. He laughed: if Melanie knew how simple this was, she'd never have bothered using him.

He spotted the hangar from a mile away, out in the open for everyone to see. Used to be part of an army base, cut deep in the ravine, hidden from prying public eyes. Part of the Cold War Era, now dried up and forgotten like himself. The Woodsman must have chosen this with a sense of irony in mind. Hide right under their noses. There were perhaps a hundred satellites in geostationary orbit over this spot, perfect for a secret uplink to the net.

He emptied his water canteen, wishing to God that it wasn't so hot. But that was Nevada. He looked for signs of occupation. He didn't want to go in there and miss the Woodsman or scare him off. There was a trail leading to the hangar entrance from some kind of small vehicle, probably a bike. The wind last night would have removed it if it wasn't recent, so he could presume the Woodsman was inside. Armed? Possibly. Dangerous? Very. He killed those guards when he escaped.

*

"I've been sent to kill you."

The Tomorrow Tower

The two men stood facing each other, Woody's eyes trying to make out features in the sunlight before he made a move. In an instant he could bring out his own gun and cut the man down, but if he was an assassin, why announce himself as such? His wrist flicked imperceptibly, and he had a palm-sized pistol pointed at the intruder.

"Drop the gun."

Buchannon dropped it. "There's little wonder you were number one."

"Sandy, check the perimeter!"

"My security systems have been over-ridden," said the computer. "Sorry," she added.

"Why didn't you tell me?"

"I did it," Buchannon said, stepping forward out of the sunlight so that Woody could see him clearly, "you're a hard man to find."

"Is it you, Buck?"

"In the flesh."

As Buchannon walked forward, there was a recognition on the Woodsman's face and puzzled relief and many questions.

"Do you really want to kill me?"

"I said that I was sent to kill you - not that I was going to carry it out."

To Buchannon, Woody looked haggard and older than his years. Yet the man was faster than he could *see*. Buchannon stepped through the memorabilia of Woody's life, seeing the pinball machines and racing games and feeling sad that Woody lived like this alone. "You've got a lot of people very angry, Woodsman."

The Tomorrow Tower

"Tomorrow they'll be even angrier."

"Yeah?"

"Tumbleweed2 will change the world as we know it."

Buchannon could see the fire in the Woodsman's eyes, the burning intensity of a man with nothing but hate and pain. So much pain.

"What's it going to do?"

"Crash and burn every military computer."

"That'll cause chaos! Deaths! Why? What reason could you have?"

"I'll show you." Woody reached into his overalls and pulled out a sachet of blue pills. "These! High-grade amphetamines that the air force made compulsory for all Stealth fighter pilots."

"You could go into rehab to get off them."

"Really? Imagine your brain pumped to fifty times its normal speed with perfect clarity of thought and reactions that you simply dream about. These pills were what helped us win the war. When you come down, you feel sluggish and dull-witted, like your head is full of glue. There's no rehab in the world that can alter that. I need pills to think! But what comes with that is the memories and I have to feel the war again and again and there's no stopping the pain, on and on. The army used me and then threw me away as a piece of human scrap addicted to blue pills. That's why I'm doing this. As a protest to show them how wrong they were to do that."

"You've changed."

"Everyone's changed."

The Tomorrow Tower

"Melanie injected me with virus so that I'd look for you to save my own skin, but I know her more than she thinks. If I kill you, she kills me. Justice. Is it true you killed three people?"

"It's true."

"The world might be a bad place, but destroying it is not the way to do it."

"I have to wipe away the memories. Have to." Woody pointed his gun at Buchannon. "You can leave now. I owe you that much."

"The war's over, has been for ten years. Look at this room! It's nothing but memories of a past that has gone. You can start again. I may be dying, but you don't have to."

"Is that why you came here? To save my soul?"

Buchannon didn't know.

"I have flown over and destroyed cities. Some civvies called it the Gulf War III, but that makes it sound like a bad sequel and they don't know what it was like. They have no idea."

"I know! Listen to me. Let me help you get off the pills and then you'll be able to live again."

"You know what it's like to fly rooftop at Mach 9? The feeling of power you get destroying a Mover before it launches missiles at thousands of people? No."

"I remember pulling you from a burning plane, my concern was for your life. I didn't know you as a person. I didn't need to know. You were another human being. Don't go and throw that back in my face."

"Please go ... or I'll shoot you."

The Tomorrow Tower

"I'm not leaving. I've nothing to lose, have you?"

Buchannon stared at Woody. There were tears in the Woodsman's eyes. He gripped the trigger and -

"PUT THE GUN DOWN!"

Melanie was at the door with half a dozen armed men. How did she get there? Woody looked at Buchannon with pure hatred. Screaming, Woody fired. Buchannon felt the blow to his chest like a sledgehammer. He stayed on his feet, feeling a tight pain and rolls of sickness. He saw Woody firing again, but at a different target. He was shooting at Melanie. Trying to kill her.

But it was Woody who flopped like his legs had been turned into liquid, dropping in a heap.

Melanie had fired first.

Buchannon looked down at his own wound. "Uh. I think I'm hit."

Melanie ran to Buchannon to stop him from falling. She had been hit in the arm. There was blood between her fingers, but she helped Buchannon sit down before he fell.

"I'm sorry for playing a dirty trick on you," she said, "but I didn't think he'd shoot you."

Buchannon grunted. "Is he dead?"

"No. Stunned."

"Why?"

"We can treat him, given time." She waved across a medic, who started treating Buchannon's wound.

"How did you find us?"

The Tomorrow Tower

"The injection I gave you contained a tracer. There was no virus present. I'd never kill you."

"So why say it and why creep into my bedroom with that weirdo?"

"You had to hate me enough to find Woody for yourself."

"You made me find him despite myself."

"Because of yourself and your damn fool sense of responsibility that makes me love you so much."

Drifting in and out of consciousness, Buchannon was lifted onto a stretcher and rushed outside. It was bright. He closed his eyes. He felt a hand squeezing his. He opened his eyes inside the ambulance to see Melanie looking down at him. She leant forward and kissed him.

"I *did* see a gun," she said.

Did it matter if he believed her?

"Forget it," he said.

Time moved on, like a tumbleweed in the wind.

RED SKY

Command 655-268

What do I most remember about the day of the moon landing? I remember my mother's hand was soft and warm. I know that sounds weird, but it's the truth.

Oh, you want to know what else?

I remember January 11th, 1969, was very, very cold. My breath formed a cloud as we walked towards the observation platform hand in hand. There were hundreds of strangers in heavy winter furs shambling around, stamping their feet on the impacted snow. I was similarly dressed in a heavy fur coat. The coat was too large and too heavy, but it fought the freezing air. Whenever my mother release my hand, I would slide them back into the long sleeves. In photographs, I look like an anorexic bear. Sniffling with cold, when I was sure no one was looking, I would wipe my red raw nose on the sleeve.

Men with thin lips and bright teeth greeted us. They all patted my head like I was a little dog. *There. There.* I kept my smile faithfully, for my father had gone to too much trouble to arrange the trip. I was nervous about meeting the people, but I was also excited to see the launch.

A man strode out of the crowd towards us. "Comrade Ruskin, I'm delighted to meet you … and your little boy."

My mother thanked him, then she tugged my arm, so we moved on, only pausing for the cameras.

"We're we going?" I asked.

"To the front, so we can see." She looked drained by the long train journey when she lit a cigarette. She was worried that it would all go wrong. We entered the VIP section. There were fifty seats, half still empty. Our names were in the middle of the front row. We sat. More people joined our row, including a fat man with a purple face, who sat down beside my mother. "Delighted to meet you. My name's Deyenkov."

"My husband says you're a genius."

Deyenkov laughed. "Only on Fridays. I take the rest of the week off."

I suppose he was being funny, but my mother didn't laugh. I could tell that she was tense. Deyenkov looked me straight in the eye. There was no warmth in his eyes. "Is this Andrei?"

"Yes!" I said.

"You look just like your mother." Deyenkov looked at his watch, too briefly to read the time. "Excuse me, but I must go to the control centre. I hope you both enjoy the launch."

"Comrade Deyenkov, the pleasure is mine."

Deyenkov walked away.

The Tomorrow Tower

"You don't like him, do you?"

"No," she said, sucking on the cigarette. "He's KGB."

"Oh," I said, not understanding.

"He's here to check up on the guests, to make sure we are not carrying bombs or copies of the New York Times." She smiled, grimly.

"Why would anyone want to carry a bomb?"

"There are all kinds of mad people in the world, Andrei. Many don't want us to succeed. Many are in the Soviet Union."

I was silent, thinking. "Is this to do with that Zond thing?"

"Hush, that's a secret. Your father should not have mentioned it." She finished the cigarette and squashed it in the ash tray provided. "Never talk about Zond in public. You could get your father and me in a lot of trouble."

"Sorry."

She smiled then and kissed me. "Forget it. Let's watch the rocket." She lifted me up and stood me on the chair, handing me some binoculars.

Suddenly Deyenkov returned. He tapped my mother on the shoulder. "I'd like you to meet Comrade Korolev. Andrei will be all right here with me, won't you?"

"Uh-huh," I said, warily.

Deyenkov took my mother's place. She walked along the row and towards a group of scientists in white coats. My mother greeted a man in a heavy grey overcoat, presumably Korolev, and then was gone.

The Tomorrow Tower

Don't say Zond, I thought. The word Zond repeated in my head and I was sure Deyenkov could read my thoughts with his cold eyes. I shivered and stared through the binoculars. I could see the massive rocket in detail and the letters CCCP on the nose cone and even the cosmonauts on the boarding platform, waiting for the word to go. One of them was my father, Captain Ivan Ruskin.

"Wave at him," Deyenkov said. "He might be able to see you."

I waved and waved, but the cosmonauts did not see me.

"Too far," he said.

I knew the other three cosmonauts: Valentina Tereshkova, Boris Yegorov and Vladimir Komarov. They had been at our home a number of times, drinking vodka and talking about space. I knew everything there was to know about the cosmonauts, from how Vladimir Komarov had almost died in Soyuz 1 to Yegorov's favourite coffee, which was the same as my mother's.

The N1 rocket was the biggest thing I had ever seen. Yes, I had seen pictures of the R-7, but this was a battleship turned to face the stars. I had imagined myself as mission captain, strapped into position at the controls, waiting for the countdown to end and the *whoosh* of the boosters, going up and up into space. Andrei Ruskin, cosmonaut, the first man on the moon. My father.

I watched the cosmonauts enter the Lunar Soyuz - LOK - and saw the platform retract. Father was inside. There was no turning back. There were a thousand different things that could go wrong and kill him. I remember thinking he might not come back. That was the first moment I was scared for him. Until then, the mission had seemed a long way away in the future.

Vehicles moved away from the launch site, and the voice of the mission control grew louder.

"... one minute to ignition ..."

I wanted to be with Mother when it launched. I looked around the platform, but the crowd had grown. I could see nothing except black hats and furs ...

"Andrei?" It was a woman. She had a pleasant oval face, bright blue eyes, and mousy brown hair. The cold reddened her cheeks. "Are you Andrei?"

"Uh-huh," I said, unsure. Who was she?

"I work with your father."

A lot of people worked with my father, I thought.

She sat in Mother's seat and said something to Deyenkov I did not hear. He shrugged, messed up my hair, and disappeared.

"What do you do?" I asked.

"I'm Leni, your father's assistant. He's told me all about you. Maybe he mentioned ... Are you enjoying the trip?"

"Yes, but ... but where's my mother gone?"

"She's got business, Andrei."

"Oh," I said. *Business.*

"Look! They are about to launch!"

I turned and faced the launch site. A siren wailed for the area to be cleared of personnel. Cameras got into position. There was a colour television housed over the platform, relaying pictures. I had never seen a colour television before.

The Tomorrow Tower

I wished Mother were with me. I wanted her warm hand, needed her warm hand. I wondered why Leni had been allowed to watch when Mother had not. That wasn't fair. What could be so important she would miss the launch?

There was a flash during the ignition and then flames gushed from the boosters. Deep thunder rippled across the ground and I felt the power in my bones. Slowly, ever so slowly, the rocket lifted, clouds of smoke obscuring the rocket until it was over my head and moving like a dart upwards, faster and faster.

"I want to be up there," I said. "Wouldn't it be fun? Can't I go next?"

Leni laughed. I couldn't see what she found funny. I was serious. "You're a bit young, Andrei."

Young! I ignored her comment. She knew nothing. My father was going to the moon and next time he would take me with him.

"Will this beat the Americans?"

"Yes - we have to beat the Americans."

The Americans. My father referred to the Americans always with a strange tone. The Americans were to be feared. Leni had the same tone.

I peered through the binoculars to follow the vapour trail left by the rocket. "How long will it take?"

"Eight days. That's there and back. It's just in time, too. There's a rumour that the Americans are to speed up the Apollo programme, but - of course - providing nothing goes wrong this week. it will be too late, won't it?"

The Tomorrow Tower

I nodded, keeping both eyes on the sky.

I was so proud of my father.

I remember much of that day, but don't remember shaking hands with General Secretary Khruzchev, something people always ask me about.

It didn't seem important at the time.

*

Three days after the launch, Mother and I were taken to the control room to see the live pictures of the landing. The pictures appeared on a large TV, the images grainy and soundless. I watched, minutes before the rest of the televised world, the broadcasts from Lunniy Korabi as it descended with its three-person crew from lunar orbit towards the grey disc. Father's voice faded in and out over the speakers. He was setting the telemetry.

The picture's quality was poor and it broke up for a worrying few seconds. It returned just before the grey surface completely filled the camera's view.

The soft landing had been smooth, but dusty as the four solid-fuel engines fired on touchdown and kicked dust sideways.

Major Komarov had been first on the ladder and an external camera showed the whole MAI-LK. The LK was green, the colour of USSR thermal paint. It was striking against the background of black sky and white lunar plains. Looking at the pictures, I wondered why I couldn't see stars. The ladder unfolded and thirty seconds passed before Komarov's orange EVA suit appeared. He waved and then proceeded carefully down the ladder. Komarov reached the bottom rung and waited for the order from Earth to proceed.

I remember Vladimir Komarov's first words as he stepped onto the grey lunar surface. I - like millions of Earthers - would never forget.

"The first great journey is over. The next has just begun for Mother Russia."

Next Father descended, letting out a cry of pleasure which caused laughter in the control room. Mother hugged me. She was crying. So was I.

*

I remember the Red Guard parade through Moscow, thousands and thousands of soldiers walking the way to the Kremlin with a huge crowd all the way and the military transport taking the MAI-LK escape pod with the cosmonauts ... and I and my mother sitting in a large car, wondering when Father could come out of quarantine ... and the cameramen and journalists, asking if we were proud to be Russians on such a momentous day ... and the helicopter that brought Father home, he was with Deyenkov and Leni ... and the tour of schools and Universities, Father answering questions from want-to-be cosmonauts ... and the tour of America, he was on TV answering the same questions a million times ... and an old lady from New York, who hated communists and tried to kill him but succeeded in wounding a television anchorman ... all these times are joined in my memory.

We lived far away from Moscow, in a house near the sea. I can't remember the name of the place, but it was hot in summer and mild in winter and our house was surrounded by trees and the nearest neighbour lived five miles away. There we would sit out at night and watch the stars and mother would cook steaks over hot coals and discuss politics. My mother was a Russian Orthodox Jew and she would tell stories of her family and the revolution. They were dissidents. She was only in the country because she had married Father.

Apollo 11 landed on the moon on the 21st of July. Neil Armstrong was the first American to step on the surface. The news was greeted with sombre acceptance. The US planned a moonbase within ten years. The newsreader said this was a direct attack on the USSR.

"Why do we hate the Americans?" I asked.

My father laughed. "We? Where did you get that idea?"

"From the news."

"Don't listen to that Krushchev propaganda. They are just like us." Father lit a cigar. "I don't hate them, but I do fear them. Their President Nixon is desperate for regaining his popularity after we beat them to the moon ... some people want the Cold War."

I did not understand. To a child, the world seemed simple. If they were like us, why did we fear them?

Nixon was impeached over the Watergate scandal and the US

changed the direction of their space initiative, setting up small manned stations, but they were years behind the Soyuz programme.

Father retired as a cosmonaut on his thirty-fifth birthday because they would not let him take another space flight. They offered him a job in the administration, which he stubbornly rejected.

"I've still got ten years in me," he said, drinking cognac from the bottle, "and they retire me because it would look bad if I got killed."

That summer he stayed in his study, drinking. I went to a school sixty miles away and came home on the weekends to a house cold and empty, despite my parents who were ghosts of their former selves. They had changed. Father would talk to nobody and Mother spent time alone, walking the beach and crying. She did a lot of crying.

I started having a strange dream. In it, Father went to the moon, where aliens were waiting for him. Little green creatures with big black slits for eyes hid in the craters. The aliens had attacked the cosmonauts, draining their humanity and replacing it with alien thoughts.

Sometimes Father would sit out looking at the stars, not moving, just looking. I would ask him what he was looking at.

"We're so small," he said, "and nobody knows it."

I occupied time with schoolwork, reading the works of Schrodinger, Heisenberg, and Hoyle, learning English and German so that I could read scientific papers in the original language. I was an eleven-year-old kid who could not talk to eleven-year-olds. Children treated me with distrust.

I was assigned a private tutor, a little woman with elephant skin, grey and wrinkled. She had blue eyes that bugged out from a thyroid problem. Miss Kadunsk. She talked in a language I could understand – mathematics.

I was dying inside, but I didn't know it, not then.

One day Father told me about the first time he saw Earth from the moon. The world was the size of a coin and disappeared behind his thumb. "When you can do that, you realise how fragile we really are."

He was talking about himself. Without the hope of going back to the moon, he was lost. He was trapped on a planet where he no longer belonged. He would drink a lot and lose his temper. I was glad to have my studies, something to think about.

When Leni came to see Father, she had become head of aeronautics at Space City. She had heard how Father was wasting away, turning into a zombie. She begged him to take the administration job because he would be able to supervise the Soyuz and MIR programmes. He accepted. That was 1976.

*

We moved to Moscow and lived on the sixth floor of an apartment building. It was hell. A bleak Stalinist concrete and brick entity thrown up in the fifties. I could just see the Kremlin from the single, tiny window of the apartment. There were no trees. I missed trees. But the apartment was convenient for Father's work. He stopped drinking at the news that Mother was pregnant and promised that everything would be all right.

Baby Valery was born in November 1977. Father and I went to the hospital, where there was a large crowd waiting. Yuri Gagarin shook Father's hand. The picture appeared on the cover of Life magazine.

Inside, the maternity ward was full of journalists. Mother was propped up in bed, holding the baby wrapped in blankets, letting photographers snap. Nurses pushed them out, leaving us alone. I kissed my mother's cheek. Father lifted the baby. She was tiny in his hands. Valery was blue-eyed and bright pink. "There are still wonders on Earth," he said.

Nine days later, little Valery died from an undiagnosed heart condition.

*

Her sudden death was a black hole nothing escaped. The apartment became claustrophobic, a prison. It was clear Mother blamed Father for the death and he felt guilty. He spent more time at Space City, working late into the night, often staying out all night. Mother stayed at home, sleeping most of each day. She would get up in the afternoon, eat a cursory meal, sitting in front of the gas heater, reading Franz Kafka. She was painfully thin and walked like an old woman. When doctors had told her that she could not have another child, the walls closed in.

Deyenkov phoned Father one day and the next I was enrolled at Moscow University studying aeronautics & astrophysics. There was no choice on my part. I was fifteen and privileged to be at the university with the older students, but I was a fish out of water.

*

The walls closed completely in late November. Father had been to Star City supervising security and had telephoned to say he'd be back at eight. I checked train timetables and discovered his train would arrive at seven, not eight, so I had gone to meet him.

I booked a cab for the return journey and waited at the Moscow train station. The train arrived and the passengers exited. He was at the far end of the platform, but Leni was with him. I waved to catch their attention, but the did not see me. Sighing, I pushed through the crowd. I was ten metres from them when Father kissed Leni, the long lingering kiss of a lover. Her arms went around him in a long embrace.

Rage filled me and I ran, ran from the platform and into the snow-filled streets. I ran the mile across the city and walked frozen and exhausted into our home. Mother saw my distress.

"What's wrong, Andrei?"

I was speechless. What could I say? She had lost Valery. I could not add to her pain with my father's betrayal. When Father arrived home forty minutes later, I had said nothing. I merely looked at him. He knew I knew.

Mother began to drink a couple of months later. She also had long arguments on the telephone with Father, who did not come home for weeks. She had vodka bottles everywhere. In the cupboards, under the sink, beneath the beds. All I could do was search for the bottles and destroy the ones I found.

Father had found her sleeping in the kitchen, clutching an empty bottle. He told me to go to bed, but I - fearing he would be violent - listened at the door.

"I stopped it months ago," his father said. "Please believe me. She meant nothing. I was weak for doing it, but it's over. I love you."

She swore and I heard glass shatter. "You did it to hurt me because of Valery's death."

"Don't talk stupid."

"You blame me."

"You can't go on drinking like this," Father said. His voice was breaking, tearful. "I don't like to see you suffer for my mistake. Please don't put yourself through this."

There were more curses and thuds and I stepped away as he heard Father come towards the door. From my bedroom, I saw him slump in a chair, holding a handkerchief against scratches on his face. Mother entered the room, swaying, holding a newly opened bottle. "Ivan, you can go to hell!"

A week later, she was found on the pavement below the apartment block, her skull shattered. She had jumped off the top

The Tomorrow Tower

floor. There were pieces of a broken vodka bottle beside her body. Father had to go to the mortuary to identify her. He never described to me what she looked like, but he wept for a week.

The funeral was a quiet ceremony with no photographers allowed. They buried Mother beside Valery. Father said a short prayer and left a single rose. I stood at the grave feeling a burning anger. Why had my mother killed herself? Did she not love me? Why had Father not prevented her from dying?

After the funeral, we travelled to a log cabin on the side of a great lake, stocked with salmon and trout. The water was a mirror. I looked into it to see my own empty face.

Father loved fishing. He had taken Mother on trips before they were married and had taught me the previous summer how to bait the hook and cast a line. I went along sullenly, loathing him for what he had done to mother. He had pushed her to kill herself, him and his stupid affair, and now he wanted to go fishing?

"Your mother was the best angler I've seen. She was a natural." Father fell into silence, walking along the water's edge to our boat. Soon, we were in the deep water, the rowing boat some quarter of a mile from shore. Father stopped rowing and lit a cigar, one given to him by Khrushchev. "Cuban," he said. "I think you're old enough to have one ..." His hand stretched out. I said no.

"Probably right. It's a bad habit."

"Could get cancer," I muttered. "Though not everyone dies that easily."

The words stung him, but I did not regret them.

The Tomorrow Tower

He sighed. "We have to talk, Andrei."

Talk? It was too late. The damage was done. I wanted to push Father into the water and then, when he surfaced, push his head under, keeping him there until he drowned. That is what I wanted to do.

Father sighed and dropped the cigar over the side. "I know you hate me. I hate me." For a long time just the gentle rocking of the boat could be heard and his husky breathing. "Do you want to know why I had an affair with Leni?"

"Because -" I hesitated. I wanted to accuse him of hating my mother. But I didn't want to say it aloud. I managed a nod and wiped my running nose. I fought back tears. "Is it because you stopped loving Mother?"

"No. Have you ever wondered why we have such a large home? Good food? Why we meet so many powerful people?"

"Because you went to the moon."

"Partly, but it's not that simple." Father was then distant, turning away to look at the water. "I didn't want you or your mother to be harmed."

"She's dead and -"

"It's my fault?"

"YES!"

"I didn't want her to hurt her. Please believe me. I never wanted an affair, but Leni is a Party member and KGB. She knew too much about me and about your mother."

"What about my mother?" I was angry and tried to stand, but

the boat wouldn't support the unbalance. I fell back, spraying us in cold water. "Tell me the truth, Father."

"Before I married her, she helped Jews leave Russia illegally. She was caught and would have gone to prison except that she was my fiance and I was a high-profile member of the space programme. I quickly married her. There was nothing they could do then if they wanted me working for them."

"That doesn't explain what you did."

"Leni knew about your mother's past. She also knew that, now that I am a lost part of history, she could use it as leverage. You see, your mother could have gone to jail as a political prisoner if I hadn't done what Leni wanted. Now she's dead, I may as well tell you everything."

"You work for the KGB, don't you?"

Father nodded, gravely.

"I practically *am* the KGB when it comes to military security with regards to space developments. I've never worked in administration. I was the first KGB man on the moon."

Father snapped his rod on his knee and threw it as far as he could. "I've done bad things, Andrei. Terrible things. Mistakes I can never forget. But there is one truth in my life. I only ever love one woman and that was your mother."

I baited my rod and swung the line into the water. About half an hour passed, neither of us saying anything.

"Andrei, can I tell you my dream?"

"I suppose so."

The Tomorrow Tower

"I dream that one day you can go into space. I'll never go into space again, but you can. I stay in the KGB because I don't want to see your dreams die the same way."

I thought of Leni at the launch of the lunar lander, pretending to be my friend. I wanted to kill her. "Leni's ruined everything!"

Father said nothing.

I wanted to die.

In 1979, I saw my chance to end everything.

Afghanistan. I joined the army against Father's wishes and against Deyenkov's and everyone who stood for the death of Mother. I wanted to die and Afghanistan offered me a chance to fulfil that wish.

I faced death on a transport driving to the capital, Kabul. Sixteen fresh-faced troops holding Kalashnikovs, swapping tall tales of love conquests. There was no danger. The convoy carried a thousand soldiers and our transport was in the middle of the line. A mortar round, probably a lucky shot, struck the road. Something whipped my face and I tasted blood. The seventeen-year-old soldier on my right had lost his head to shrapnel. It was his blood I was covered with. He had stolen the bullet with my name on it.

There was a fire-fight in the hills. Mujahedeen guerillas were taking shots at one of the Russian roadblocks, killing two soldiers. I volunteered to root them out. My commanding officer knew I had a deathwish, so he didn't want to be around when I died, so he sent me out alone. I climbed a crag, getting above the sniper. I waited for a movement and trained my assault rifle on a child no older than twelve. He was carrying a WWII rifle. I had him in my sights for an hour. I watched him eat a meagre meal and defecate. He was just a child with a gun protecting his country. I aimed and fired. The bullet missed. The child ran, forgetting his gun in the panic. I went down, collected the weapon, and returned to the base. I said the sniper was dead, and because I had the gun and the shooting had stopped, they believed me. There would be no search. The child would live another day, but if he chose to pick up another rifle then so be it.

My tour ended. I gave my medals away to a woman and baby I encountered at Moscow station whose husband had died in the war.

Father wanted me to return with him to his new apartment. It was bigger and better, he promised. I said no.

Instead, I lived in a one-room flat that smelled of dry rot and vegetables. I worked briefly as a translator for US and English visitors. The pay was low, but there were always roubles to be made on the black market selling cigarettes. I would lie awake at night, listening to the life in the walls, cockroaches and beetles in complex mating rituals, and dream.

*

I remember the Viking pictures: the bright white-pink sky; the brown rocks and boulders; the miles of an alien land. They had triggered something in my unconscious mind that surfaced in dreams. A doorway had opened. I was standing on rust-coloured soil and walking across Martian dunes, wearing a hard-suit made from light alloys and plastics that offered freedom of movement. I could feel the EVA suit and the icy breaths of air. It was real. I'd wake knowing I had stepped on Mars; I felt the extra pull of Earth's gravity as a palpable thing, like pulling myself out of a swimming pool.

I had to go there. I knew it as surely as Sir Edmund Hillary knew he had to climb Everest and Father had to go to the moon.

Deyenkov was surprised to see his reluctant pupil return. "Had enough of war?" he asked.

"For many lifetimes," I said.

I continued studying astronautics, engineering, and computer science, working on design improvements for the MIR space stations.

Meanwhile, the US started to look seriously at Mars. Mars offered them a way to get ahead. One Brezhnev could not ignore.

The Space Race to Mars began.

*

1983. I heard that my father was taken ill. Apparently whatever he did for the KGB was better served by a younger man (or woman). KGB privileges let him live in the lake retreat permanently.

1984. Deyenkov made me his assistant. I was given access to high-security files, where I discovered that our space programme had suffered a number of setbacks, mainly financial support.

I learned that my father was now living with Leni. She was looking after him during his illness.

The Tomorrow Tower

1985. Father had cancer. Some malignant intestinal variety. Incurable. It was Leni who told me over the phone he had a week left. She was crying. In a strange way, I felt sorry for her. Father wanted to see me one last time. I drove three hundred miles overnight, parking at the lodge as in the early light of dawn. Leni led me inside. Father was surrounded by medical equipment and on a morphine drip. He was awake and attempted a smile, I saw the bones in his neck and the stretch of paper skin.

"Payback, son. I owe your mother an agonizing death, eh? Can't even smoke without it hurting."

"Dad, I didn't know."

"I ... didn't want you to know. You were doing so well with your career ... didn't want to you to play nursemaid to a dying man." He coughed weakly. I held his hand. Leni started crying.

"Remember I love you," I said, my mother's words echoing.

"I'm sorry," he said. His face distorted and he grunted with pain. "Andrei?" His eyes were blank, unfocused.

"I'm still here, Dad."

"Never ... forget your dreams."

"I won't," I promised.

Father coughed painfully. Leni adjusted the drip until he passed out. I walked outside.

*

1986. Death was 72 seconds. Francis Scobee. Michael J Smith.

The Tomorrow Tower

Ellison S Onizuka. Judith A Resnik. Ronald E McNair. S Christa McAuliffe. Gregory B Jarvis. The 51-L Challenger crew. How many others remember their names?

*

"What are you thinking about?"

I was startled out of my recollection. I had forgotten about the experiment and must have wasted a good few minutes. Embarrassed, I turned and faced the speaker. It was Bachovich. Bachovich had somehow crept up on me unannounced. He held onto the roof rail, using one hand to hold a juice concentrate that he sucked through the nozzle. Bachovich was the only person I knew who liked the taste of the urine-coloured liquid. He asked his question again.

"I was just remembering the moon landing," I lied. "I was only eight. Seems like yesterday."

"I wasn't born then," Bachovich said. "You're a real old-timer, Ruskin."

I nodded. I was forty-one, but I was still in good condition. I had to be good to pass the tests. Bachovich was twenty.

"My time in the gym is it?" I asked.

"Forgotten the schedule as well?" Bachovich grinned. "Fourteen hundred hours . It's a shift change."

"I know," I said, "but that experiment dulls the mind."

I unbuckled the harness and swung round towards the hatchway. Bachovich squeezed by and replaced me. Then I entered the hub and finally 'down' the narrow tunnel to the gym.

Henkoff was in the exercise module, grinding his leg muscles against the machine. He popped a steroid boost - to hell with hormonal imbalances - and grunted. His legs were on fire. "Hey, Andrei, you look like you need a vacation. Why don't you step outside for some fresh air, eh?"

"Those pills will put hair in places it shouldn't be - say, between your ears."

Henkoff puffed and increased his speed. His face was a deep crimson. "Stansky used these to break eight seconds for the hundred metres, so I heard."

"Yeah, long as the Olympics drug officials don't. Go easy on it, comrade."

"Huh," mumbled Henkoff. "Have to ... keep going."

I grabbed the arm restraints and began my aerobics session, watching the heart rate and respiratory readings as I built up speed. Henkoff started talking about the benefits of steroids (between grunts) and I tried my best to ignore him.

I finished my physical training, sheathed in sweat and ready for a long shower. Unfortunately, I would have to make do with a cool air-dry via vacuum hose. On my way to the chamber, I looked through a viewport: Mars was a day away. I marvelled at the red planet.

After 'showering' I went to the sleep quarters. The four bunks were empty: the whole crew was required to be active during the test phase. It was not time for the sleep period and - as we approached

The Tomorrow Tower

Mars - the next would be on the surface. No, what I sought was in my private locker, where I had the few personal possessions allowed on the payload. I removed the bronze urn - sneaked aboard in my hygiene effects - and wondered if I was being foolish for bringing it. Yes. I heard a noise and pushed the urn back into its place, closed the locker and locked it.

"So," said Henkoff, emerging from his quarters in a clean orange uniform, "you actually remember the first moon landing?"

"I was at the parade in Red Square for when they got back. I even got to shake hands with Khruzchev, twice."

"No kidding? How could you do that?"

"My father was an important man."

"I forgot - the second man on the moon and all that. Say, what happened to him?"

"Things," I said.

Bad things.

*

I have fits of depression because two-and-a-half years on board a cramped spaceship have focused my memories, gnawing away at me. I considered destroying the Mars lander - a few rewired circuits would be enough. But what would death in space achieve? Just a setback and more lost lives.

I entered a NASA archive and typed access codes that opened files on the early Mercury and Apollo flights. I searched their astronauts' logs, looking for answers. It was something Leni had said in 1969. *We have to beat*

The Tomorrow Tower

the Americans. The thought repulsed me. Leni, in her naivety, had summarised the problem. She had indirectly killed his mother with her misguided love.

I found what I wanted and wrote it down and practised the American phrase. I hoped a few simple words would be enough to start the healing process.

Garassi, Henkoff and Bachovich had been chosen for the primary drop from the seventy cosmonauts trained for long-haul flights. The MIR-2000 landing craft entered the Martian atmosphere, jerking in the turbulence. Emergency systems M289-M304 blurted out angry warnings.

"We've lost a heat shield," shouted Henkoff over the noises in the vibrating cabin. "Hull temperature rising."

Bachovich read out the temperature readings, still within the safety margins, but higher than expected. Entry into the upper atmosphere had its risks, but there was nothing we could do if the heat shields failed. G-forces increased and the ESM310 lit. Another heat shield had gone.

I looked at Bachovich for a report. Bachovich said we were near burn up. I responded by activating the retros and the craft juddered unhealthily against the deceleration. Then we were through the tough stuff.

I ejected the parachute and Henkoff confirmed it was working. All it required for a soft landing were short bursts from the boosters to slow the descent and the computers handled the rest. We landed at 12.04.32 Moscow time.

Henkoff and Garassi rerouted a few damaged circuits and swore several times before confirming the landing had been rough but basically by the numbers.

The Tomorrow Tower

Bachovich switched on the external monitors and the foursome stared at the red planet. We had landed in position A, one hundred metres from the automated base Colony One that had been constructed by the now idle vehicles to our right. I saw the biosphere's outer hatchway ahead and the USSR flag waving in the Martian wind. We were so adrenalin-pumped that nobody considered smiling.

"Home," muttered Henkoff.

I connected my helmet and air tanks and took the urn from my clothes. It was just like my dream. The pink sky welcomed. Henkoff's utterance had been correct. This was home. My three comrades patted my back, and I climbed into the airlock for depressurisation.

An interminably long time later, the main hatch opened and bright sunlight flooded in. Martian daylight.

Checking my helmet camera, I realised that the people back on Earth were seeing what I saw, billions of eyes looking through mine.

I stepped forward and climbed out to the first leading down to the surface.

I knew what it must have been like for Father in 1969, doing something never done before. I descended with barely concealed hurry, but I stopped on the final one.

I paused and tipped Father's ashes into the wind and I uttered the words of another dreamer.

"This is one small step for a man, one giant leap for mankind."

REALITY

GAMES

A year passed before it was safe to visit Earth.

"I always get nervous," said the shuttle passenger sitting next to Rick. "That's why I'm armed to the teeth."

Rick took his eyes off the blackness of space to look at the traveller. The guy looked like a soldier from Vietnam. He was wearing khaki combat fatigues bulging with grenades, plus a wicked dagger and a pump-action shotgun. On his lap, he clutched a mini-Bible New Millennium Edition and a copy of the Koran. Also, a blood-stained encyclopaedia. As if that wasn't strange enough, his clothes were too big for him.

Rick felt seriously under-dressed. "Why are you dressed like that?"

"Man, you can't take no chances out there."

"You're nervous," Rick said, "dressed like that?"

"I'd be stupid not to be. Sure, I'll feel better once we get into the sphere of influence. But right now I got the jitters." The man patted the belt of grenades with something like affection. "These babies assure some protection against the more dangerous ideas. The Bible and other stuff are to ward off paranormal evil. It's all psychological, man. Say, this your first time home since The Breakdown?"

Rick nodded. "I was working on Mars, in the mines. I didn't hear about the disaster until a couple of days ago. They don't allow communicators. My family's down there on Earth, trapped."

The man poked him hard in the chest.

"Hey!"

"Where's your body armour, eh?"

"I didn't think I'd need any."

"Living on the edge, huh? Got to admire your guts, man."

"Is it really that bad?"

"Yep. And then some." A smug grin. "Say - we ain't been introduced. They call me Red on account of my beard."

"But your beard's not red."

"It soon will be."

"Well, I'm glad to meet you, Red." Rick always sat next to the weirdo on long journeys. "They call me Rick on account of that's my name."

"Where you from, Rick?"

"New England."

"New England, huh? I had a buddy who lived in Maine. Dude died in The Breakdown, but that's bad luck for him, right? Should have been real careful, that's what I say. Maine's full of Stephen

The Tomorrow Tower

King's stories given flesh. Killer clowns, rabid dogs, psychotic cars, vampires ... Those writer guys are responsible for a lot of killing."

"If it's so bad, what are you going back for?"

"There's money to be made from dream merchandise, man."

"Oh," Rick said, not understanding what Red was talking about. His knowledge of The Breakdown was technical, not practical. He knew there had been a leakage of nanomachines into the air and their quantum computers were the first sentient generation. He also knew that with no set rules for replication. The nanomachines had gone wild, absorbing everything. After just a few minutes, the whole Earth had become one huge network of nanomachines, all competing for dominance. He knew that. And it worried him. Human minds had merged with the machine to form one massive dreamscape. Now any thought could be transform into a physical reality, with the result that the normal reality collapsed into billions of over-lapping consensus bubbles. But what did that mean in layperson's terms? He didn't know.

"Last time I was in Thailand, I picked up a living effigy of Buddha," Red said. "No joke. Solid gold. All philosophical, he was. Incredible."

"Fantastic," Rick muttered. "Look, Red, I'm not sightseeing or out to collect treasures. My wife and kids are on Earth, and I want to find them. Can you help?"

"Word of advice, buddy. Hold on to your own thoughts. Don't let those suckers mess with your mind. Many folks were killed when the consensus reality crashed and burned, but, as long as you play by the new rules of the game, you should be fine. Say - why don't you forget the past and find yourself a new girlfriend? Ever wanted Marilyn Monroe or Madonna?"

"No."

"Man, why settle for one when you could have a harem of dream girls? Think about it."

"I want my family," Rick said. He turned and stared out of the window. From lunar distance, the Earth looked normal, the friendly marble he loved. Blue and white and homely. He wondered what it would be like nearer the consensus reality field.

"They're bound to be dead," Red said. "It's no big deal. You don't have to be the same person here. My nag-nag wife got wasted in the first hour. Best thing that ever happened to me."

That didn't surprise Rick. His family was probably dead, too, like the jerk said.

"WARNING! YOU ARE ENTERING CONSENSUS REALITY BREAKDOWN!"

"Hold on to -" Red was interrupted. The rest of his sentence was lost in the maelstrom of sights and sounds and screams that accompanied the transition. One second there was the reality Rick was used to and the next -

And the next he was sitting next to a young Arnold Schwarzenegger, with a beard. "Ain't that amazing, man?" Arnie said without a trace of an Austrian accent. He was wearing the same clothes and weapons as Red, but they fit Arnie properly. "Rick, be what you wanna be. Do what you wanna do!"

The Tomorrow Tower

"How did you -" Rick saw the other passengers and stopped talking. Many had changed into people he recognised. Famous people. An Elvis Presley. Three JFKs. A James Bond. Some had altered subtly, say, lost a few pounds or gained a pate of healthy hair. He wondered what he himself looked like. He asked a carbon copy of Queen Elizabeth II if she had a mirror. She said she had. A jewelled hand passed a gold vanity mirror. Rick studied himself. He looked the same tired self he had seen on Mars this morning. He sighed with relief, took some deep, deep breaths and looked around for further changes in reality.

The shuttle looked normal, but up close there were differences. The emergency sign over his head (which nobody ever read) had altered into half-formed gibberish in an alphabet that didn't exist. It was blurred the same way he saw things without his contact lenses. He realised it was what he perceived the notice to be, not what should have been. This world was in a state of flux, dependent on the memories of everyone in it for its realism. And his family had been left alone while he had been on Mars. He'd left them to work on a two-year contract, to improve their standard of living, just like oil riggers had done a few centuries ago. The thought that he would never see them again hurt like a blow to the chest.

He felt a blow to the chest.

"Easy, man," Arnie/Red said, "what did I tell you about rogue thoughts? Concentrate or you'll kill yourself."

"Concentrate. Okay, I'm concentrating. I'm concentrating on keeping sane."

The Tomorrow Tower

"Keep trying. You might get there."

*

The New York spaceport terminal was aptly named. Massive queues stretched on to infinity. A guard rail separated the area and the words 'KEEP OUT: Reality Blackspot' warned against going too close. Rick could see why. Over the perimeter, the people were queuing in a Stalinist bleakness. Cobwebs had collected on their drab clothes. Some people, mostly old people with sad, sad looks, had died in the line and were decomposing into skeletons. The rest of the queue seemed not to notice this atrocity.

"What's wrong with those people?"

He received an answer from the Trans-World Rep. "They were caught in the terminal when the nanomachines escaped. Their expectations of how long a delay they'd have to wait have trapped them forever. Collectively, they are keeping each other in the bubble of consensus. Effectively, time is as slow as it gets."

"Those people are dying."

"Afraid you're right. But don't try to help, sir. You'll get caught in the same depressing reality. Follow me through the green channel and you'll be okay. There are no delays unless you feel guilty."

"If I feel guilty -"

"You'll get the worst body cavity search in history, sir."

"I don't feel guilty. Honest."

"Sir, this area is sort of the opposite of over there. The

145

company hires optimists only, now, as a matter of law. No delays. No psychoses. The green channel works on time - it's what people believe, so it has become true." The Rep moved him along to collect his luggage. Rick was through the terminal and in the daylight before he had another dark thought. New York in all its brightness exploded. This is a grim world, he thought. Heaven and hell thrown together by a madman.

There was a gentle shifting of things, the ground, the buildings, the sky, as if somebody was painting a watercolour on a roller coaster. When the artist slipped a stroke, the break in reality was noticeable in small ways. When consensus reality was under a microscope, it was ephemeral as an electron's position. Where mixed memories of the local area combined, the reality stayed fixed and concrete. The Statue of Liberty, engraved on the nation's consciousness, was unfalteringly solid and crisp. More so than before, he reckoned. Weird.

"Hey, man, what you waiting for?" Red said, appearing beside him, pushing him towards the street.

"Huh?"

"Do you know where you're going?"

"I need to get to Boston. I'll get a cab."

A yellow cab streaked out of nowhere. The taxi driver shoved his head out of the window. He looked like Robert De Niro. "You talking to me? You talking to me?"

"Whoa! Easy now!" Red said. "Don't do that, Rick. In this world all cab drivers are psychos."

The Tomorrow Tower

"That's a stereotype."

"Stereotypes live here, man. How many times do you see Robert De Niro driving a cab? My advice is to get a bus." Red pointed down the street. "Oh, avoid the subway, too. It's deadly. Got to go hunting, man." He grinned. "I'll be back." Red readied his shotgun and strolled down the block.

Rick heard shots being fired.

Red was apparently enjoying himself.

Rick set off into the city.

*

Suddenly -

The street was sucked away to be replaced by bright neon strips flickering over a fractal landscape. His neurones blended in an infinite data stream.

1010100111111101010101010101010010101

1100000110010100100001111000011001

110000100010

11001001

"What the hell is this?" Rick was standing on an infinite green PCB board that dwarfed him. Above, towers of electric blue snaked between towers of pulsating data. Computer programs that looked like shiny ice in the midday sun shifted at the speed of light. His surprise and confusion spider-webbed from his head as binary numbers and joined the data currents. Far off, huge chips and resistors from a bygone era flickered with golden surfaces, devouring smaller components.

He thought: cyberspace.

No, not cyberspace. *I'm in someone's idea of cyberspace.* Jesus. This is insane. This is over the top. He felt cables running down his face like sweat and the weight of a VR helmet. William Gibson eat your heart out. This is way over the top.

WHO ARE YOU?

The voice hit him violently, reverberating around his head like a gunshot.

Rick thought he said his name aloud, but didn't hear the word. But he did see it, floating like a hologram a thousand miles high.

RICK. MY NAME IS RICK.

RICK? WHO'S RICK?

Rick moved forward, hoping to find the source of the voice. But everything moved away as he approached, like an unfolding carpet.

Then he saw the dragon. Hard-edged, plastic and chrome. Two glass eyes and a mouth filled with steel razors. Body lacquered with metallic plating. It swooped gracefully from the data clouds, black ice bellowing from its lungs.

This couldn't be happening.

YOU DO NOT BELONG HERE.

The dragon descended maniacally. The impact would flatten Rick into a pulp. No where to run.

"Forget this," Rich shouted. He reached up and grabbed either side of the helmet and pulled. He jacked out -

The Tomorrow Tower

And found himself cowering on the sidewalk.

He stood and brushed the dust off his clothes. There was a pimply youth sleeping in a doorway with a battered copy of William Gibson's Neuromancer in his hands. He'd been inside the kid's dream. The kid was petulantly saying "Rick" over and over, as if he was angry that Rick had escaped.

This could be a very dangerous place, Rick thought.

*

Rick reached the Greyhound Station after a long trek through several dangerous neighbourhoods. A bag lady, living in an alcoholic stupor, had led him into a squalid city of narrow alleys and nasty people. He broke free of her consensus bubble and nearly broke his nose on the pole of a streetlight. So he was wary and dishevelled when he finally paid the fare to Boston and boarded the bus. The bus was an old-fashioned one. It needed wheels and ran on gas. It was as if his childhood memories had formed it.

It was packed with oddball stereotypes: junkies, pregnant women about to give birth, angry teenagers with spiky hair and attitudes. The kind of people in old television shows. He squeezed down the aisle and found an empty row and stretched out his feet so no one could sit next to him. For once, his tiredness was in his imagination and manifesting itself as genuine muscle aches. He fought the feeling.

Mounted on a retractable screen was a TV. He switched it on,

The Tomorrow Tower

curious to see if it worked. He was surprised that it did. The world could end, but TV was immortal. The multitude of channels showed the usual dross, but some programmes possessed an eerie quality. He watched a TV evangelist shriek at an audience of seven, eight thousand believers. Bobby Lou Jackson of the Fellowship of Christian Worship got some very ill people on the stage and then proceeded to cure them. Rick saw genuine faith healing.

"Praise the Lord! Repent your sins for only 99 dollars!"

A coldness seeped through him. Other faith programmes were similarly miraculous. It was chilling.

Then Rick located a news broadcast. Atrocities in the Middle East: Islamic Fundamentalists executing 'heathens.' Atrocities in Eastern Europe: Christian Fundamentalists executing 'heathens.' Prime Time shows investigating the increase in Nazis in Berlin - with the Fourth Reich and a Hitler reborn from nightmares. Poltergeists. UFOs. The Loch Ness monster. Real in the minds of some people. Now real in the minds of everyone.

He didn't want to see more, so he switched off.

The bus was crossing typical New England scenery. Typical? Stereotypical. He noticed the smoky, sweaty smell vanishing as if someone had sprayed a giant air freshener into the bus. Golden brown and scarlet leaves carpeted the small towns he passed through. Towns that looked suspiciously like an amalgam of every small town in America, an America of the 1950s. He watched elms trees shedding rose-tinted leaves.

It was autumn – in the middle of June.

The Tomorrow Tower

The gentle caress of the air conditioner lulled him asleep. He woke when his head jerked against the window. The bus was going up a hill covered with lush forest. Now he was the only passenger. A Methodist church emerged out of the oaks, the spire glimmering in the sunlight. In the valley below, the small town of Blackwell clung to the meandering river. Home, he thought. The bus stopped and the driver unpacked his bags. Rick thanked him - and the bus disappeared. Maybe the idea was no longer needed?

Blackwell was an obscure suburb of Boston. He wondered how the driver had known where he lived. Weird, he thought. He walked down tree-lined avenues, breathing the lavender air. He smiled at the red squirrels that popped up from among the leaves, nut collecting, scampering tree to tree. He thought he saw one wink at him.

He was a block from his house when he realised something was missing. It was so obvious he let out a cry. No people!

Nobody. He ran up a driveway where two matching '58 Cadillacs were parked. He pressed the bell. He waited, peering through the stained glass at the dark shapes in the hall. There was nobody in. He tried another and another and another and -

His town was empty.

He sprinted home. Outside on the lawn were Tim's push-bike and Hazel's dolls. Rick sneezed and realised the grass had been cut. So, it hadn't been abandoned. He went to the door and fumbled a key card out of his wallet and unlocked it. Inside, he heard voices.

"Liz? Hazel? Tim?"

He entered the lounge and found it empty. Clean, but empty.

The Tomorrow Tower

Panic filled him. Maybe Red was right, maybe they were dead. But he had heard voices. He searched in vain for the source of the sound. Each room was the same. Empty. Where were they? He couldn't believe they were dead. He returned to the lounge, slumped on the sofa, and wept.

"They can't be dead. I'd feel it. I'd know it."

Rick checked the table next to the phone. He flicked through unpaid bills. A letter from Harvard caught his interest. His wife had worked in the School of Computer Psychology, and the letter was a notice from a colleague, Dr Kaver, dated a year ago. Rick remembered Peter Kaver as a decent guy. And he lived nearby. Perhaps the computer psychologist could tell him what had happened in Blackwell? He hoped so. He opened the car and was pleased to see the antique Fiat that Liz had bought on her tour of Europe. He drove it to Kaver's apartment. Rick could see a few people walking around the streets, chatting as if everything was okay.

Kaver answered the door in baggy corduroy pants and a crumpled polyester shirt. His bleary eyes narrowed. "Rick, what are you doing here?"

Not the greeting Rick expected. "I've just got back from Mars."

"I gathered that."

He heard someone inside. A woman who sounded like his wife.

Rick made a move to enter the apartment, but Kaver blocked his path. "Who have you got in there?"

"What do you mean?"

"There's somebody in there."

The Tomorrow Tower

"No, there's not." Kaver began rolling up his sleeves. The threat was obvious.

"Let me in, Kaver, you've got my wife in there -"

"Are you accusing me of having an affair with Liz?"

"Liz? You're awfully familiar."

"You're paranoid."

"Are you letting me in or not?"

"Not." Kaver stepped back and attempted to close the door. Rick pushed forward into the room. He smelt laundry and diapers. Kaver grabbed him, but he shrugged him off. The apartment was a mess, as though thirty people lived in one room. He heard the woman in the kitchen.

"Don't go in there," Kaver said.

Rick ignored him. As he entered, he became entangled in a load of wet clothes hanging from a washing line. Tearing himself loose, he saw there was an ironing board in front of him. A bedraggled woman in a blue apron slaved over a mound of polyester shirts. Rick barely recognised his wife. Liz looked fifty years old. Yet she was bloated with pregnancy. She worked at the ironing while three babies gurgled in a cot under the sink. Kaver caught up with Rick.

"She's mine now! You can get out of here!"

"Is this what you fantasised about? Is this domestic hell your idea of marriage? What have you done?"

"I haven't done anything. You left her alone and she needed me. That's all." Kaver produced a marriage certificate from his pocket. "See? Your marriage was annulled and now she's my girl."

153

The Tomorrow Tower

"I don't believe this. Look at her. She's a slave."

Liz looked up from the laundry and asked Kaver if there was anything else she could do for him? Make dinner? It was as if Rick was invisible. Kaver told her to finish the ironing first. She obeyed. "See, she loves me now."

Rick's anger exploded. "I come home and I find you using my wife as a doormat! How do you think that makes me feel?"

"She loves me. Can't you see the truth? Watch!" He turned to Liz. "Honey, do you love me?"

"Yes, sweetie-pie!" she said in a girlish voice. Rick had never heard Liz talking like that before. She doted on the creep.

"That thing isn't my wife, Kaver. Liz is an independent, intelligent woman. That thing is a parody of the perfect wife. Did you watch the Stepford Wives on TV and take it too seriously? Come on, what have you done?"

Kaver's face shared a dozen emotions, ranging from anger to a straining bowel movement. Liz flickered like a candle. Kaver saw it too and opened his mouth in a big O. "Stop it!"

Liz, the babies, the ironing board and the rest of the domestic nightmare warped and twisted and rapidly faded. They were left in a normal room, just Rick and Kaver facing each other like gunslingers. That thought produced Smith and Wesson 45's in their hands. Kaver dropped it as if hot. "Don't shoot me." He shook head to foot.

Despite Rick's disgust at what Kaver had done with his wife dissolved, he felt sorry for the sad man and his pathetic dream. Even his dream had been woefully inadequate.

The Tomorrow Tower

"What have I done?" Kaver wept blood, literally. "I am useless."

Rick didn't say anything in agreement, despite the temptation. He needed the psychologist's help. "Peter, you have to help me. I need to find the real Liz."

"Real? I don't know what's real these days. Is this room real? Are you? Am I?"

"Peter, think back to the day of The Breakdown. Tell me what happened."

"What happened? What didn't happen? Santa Claus came down my chimney, that's what. And I don't have a chimney. What's real and what's not? Is that the question?" Kaver was dazed after losing his pseudo-family. "You should have seen the chaos. You know what? My department even had a part in the mistake. We were trying experiments on some rats, giving them a dose of the sentient nanomachines. Did you know rats dream?"

"No."

"They do. Unfortunately, they dreamt of a hole in their cage. The rats escaped. The nanomachines multiplied out of the lab. It was crazy. A lot of people died in the seconds after the consensus broke down simply because they didn't believe in themselves and de-existed. I don't think, therefore I don't exist. Goodbye existence!"

"Is that what happened to Liz?"

"Liz? I don't know. I thought ... I don't know what I thought."

You thought she loved you. "What happened to my kids?"

"I don't know. Look, I expect they de-existed."

"They're dead?"

155

"Yes and no. Or rather they might be *both*. Think about it. Have you seen any children?"

"No."

"Exactly. Either their concepts of the world are too immature to maintain them in our reality or they are still here and we can't see them, isolated in their own consensus bubbles."

"I don't understand. Are you saying they are dead or alive?"

"I've seen many people caught in their own bubbles. Some may be invisible in the general world consensus. This part of the universe is now flexible. The laws of physics can do just about anything."

"Great, thanks a lot."

As Rick left Kaver, he noticed the reappearance of a family photograph. Kaver, Liz and their babies were in a loving embrace. Sighing, Rick left quickly before Kaver's fantasy fully formed again.

Back at the house, Rick searched for clues to where his family had disappeared to. He checked everything inside and out, reading letters three times over, looking for clues. Nothing. He removed clothes from wardrobes and stepped inside in case a Narnia-type place had been created.

Nothing.

He despaired at the lack of information he possessed. A year had passed and there was nothing to show for it. He picked Liz's new clothes from the melee and started putting them back in her drawers, for want of nothing better to do. He stopped. New clothes? Yes, a dress he hadn't seen before. Some blouses. He'd found a glitch. New clothes meant -

The Tomorrow Tower

- meant it was not part of his conscious self.

So Liz was alive!

(But where?)

He ran to Liz's study and to the computer that she had used to keep in constant contact with the university. Leafing through her notebook, he found the password: Reality Games. He told the computer to call Boston University. He got through to the AI, affectionately nicknamed Bubba (Boston University Big BrAin). Bubba's artificial reality was fixed in the 'normal' reference world and still functioned as expected. Thank the God of Machines, he thought.

"What can I do for you, Mr Taylor?"

What did he want?

"Access the notes from Dr Kaver and my wife's studies up to their last entry."

"Done. What do you need to know, Mr Taylor?"

"Tell me what happened to the people who disappeared."

Bubba considered this for a long time. "Nobody has disappeared to my knowledge."

"Not to your knowledge?" He was losing his temper with the AI. Bubba detected the speech altercation and told him that it was true that the department of computer psychology had been unused by many of the pre-disaster personnel, but the disappearances were not real but imaginary.

"Are you saying I'm crazy?"

"No, according to my analysis, this is to be expected. Children during their early development have different cognitive abilities. They are only aware of what they have experienced. They now live in the bubbles they have created. Your wife, being part of two such similar minds, should exist in the overlapping bubbles of Hazel and Tim. It is this reality which is closed to you because you were not present when the consensus broke down."

"What can I do about it?"

"What do you want to do about it?"

"That's all, Bubba," he said. He sat for a long time. Were Liz and the children occupying the same space but in a different conscious layer? The nanomachines could regulate the senses perceived. Was he the blind one? He walked outside and touched Tim's push-bike; the little red plastic vehicle was his son's favourite toy. Did Tim play with it now?

Rick walked around the house to the garden and sat on the bench he had made two summers ago. He had sat with the twins on his lap and told them stories. The toddlers had listened to every word, enraptured. He sat until dark, neither thinking nor feeling. The stars twinkled into existence. Staring for a long time at the firmament, he saw individual galaxies and stars in those galaxies. It was like an astrophotograph in detail and beauty. How was that possible? Was he imaging it or was the Earth giving him the skills to see further?

He closed his eyes and wished that Liz, Tim and Hazel were with him. If he wanted something so much, could it really happen?

Could it happen? Could it? COULD IT?

The Tomorrow Tower

I WANT MY LIFE BACK!

And he could visualise it, the world where Tim and Hazel and his wife Liz still lived.

*

Rick felt a tugging of his wrist and a tiny, smooth hand in his own.

"Daddy, can we play?"

He opened his eyes to a new day. The sky was blue. He was in a meadow that he had last visited in his own childhood, where he'd spent many idle days chewing grass stalks, watching cotton-wool clouds reshape above. Today there was a gentle breeze and the smells of spring. Hazel and Tim went off to play with their kites. The picnic was good. Life was good. Rick vaguely remembered a life without his family, and he felt sadness. The past was not for him.

Liz stood with her back to the sun. She was radiant and young again, just the way he remembered. "Is it you?"

At first, he did not know what she meant.

"Yes," he said.

She cocked her head and smiled. "I've dreamt about you," she said, "and so have the kids. We knew you'd come back. This picnic was their idea."

"Is this real?"

"Is what real?"

"This."

"Don't be silly, Rick. Pass me a sandwich."

The Tomorrow Tower

He passed one. "Is this what our children dream?"

She shrugged and then bent down to kiss him on the cheek. "Does it matter? Anything is possible." A rainbow appeared above them, even though there was no water vapour to create it. "Lovely day, isn't it?"

"Just like I remember," Rick said. "I hope it stays this way forever."

"It will," Liz replied. They looked at the kids playing, and Rick knew the year would be one long summer full of pleasant memories.

You see, that was the consensus.

NEW BABYLON

A Western multimedia journalist once described Santari's palace as the 'New Babylon for the New Millennium.' As Santari stood on the highest balcony, admiring his Great Pyramid far below, he considered the statement an insult typical of a small-minded man. His palace was far greater than that ancient construction. The world's best nanoengineers and biotechnicians had created for his pleasure the ultimate in abodes - a building responsive to his touch, to his mood, shaping itself to whatever he wished - and yet people compared it to a dead thing, a thing that no longer existed. It angered him. Why did ordinary people always make an example of the past when only the future could changed.

He did not know or care.

That was a lie.

He did care deeply.

He stared at the Great Pyramid, fists clenched.

The Great Pyramid was an expression of his distaste for the limited minds of his inferiors by harking back to the days before nanotechnology made construction a mere computer exercise. His

161

palace may have been built in a day, but the pyramid was something requiring time and effort. He liked to think of it this way: A man could have a computer write a novel using the parameters of his choosing - length, style, plot, characters - but how much greater was the satisfaction of writing it himself, word by word, page by page, discovering it as he wrote? It was the same with his pyramid. A work of blood, sweat, and tears. And soon it would be finished. No one could say that it was just another nanotech building. No one.

Santari could see the human workers crawling over the Eighth Wonder of the World, chiselling out the greatest achievement of the century. Their noise was rhythmical, as he had ordered. He abhorred noise, so the work was done musically. The pyramid was twice the dimensions of its Egyptian namesake. Impressively, none of it had been built using the despised Japanese nanotech architects. The effort was important. It was not an achievement to hire Japanese nanotechnology. No. Each stone had been hewn by human hand from Egyptian rock and be transported across the oceans by sea, not air. According to the multimedia releases, it was a memorial tomb for those who died in Zarabi's first (and last) civil war in 2037. Santari smiled: If only the Outside World knew its true purpose.

His weblink bleeped. He looked at his wrist and saw the youthful face of General Malawi. After the terrorist bombing of his old palace, there were many new faces in his Cabinet, colonels raised in rank to generals. Malawi was one of them. He looked too young for the five-star uniform. He'd barely grown a moustache. But he was loyal.

The Tomorrow Tower

"Sir, the ambassadors have arrived. Should I send them up?"

"Do so."

Waiting, Santari watched his thousands of gardeners working on the pyramid's surface. They had started work six months ago at the bottom, adding slow-grown plants and flowers, layer by layer. Now they were close to the top. Similarly, engineers had constructed rainbow waterfalls and glorious pools that glinted like the surface of a mirror, all crafted at the slow pace of humans. The engineers worked diligently. Idly, he wondered how many had loyalty implants.

In two days, his devoted army would finish a platinum statue of him on the pyramid's apex for the populace to admire. A feeling close to bliss filled Santari as he closed his eyes and felt the sun on his face. But his mood darkened, recalling the terrorist bombing that had killed his two sons and himself. His memory engrams had been patterned into a new body, a body now reshaped to look like the original Santari, but his sons had been closer to the blast. Their brains had been pulped by the explosion. If only Vashmir and Kassan were standing beside him, he would be complete. But all he felt was unease.

He heard the chatter of the ambassadors as they left the elevator and took their first look at the Great Pyramid. They gaped like slack-jawed monkeys. Santari inwardly smiled. Fools.

"Gentlemen ... and ladies ... what you see is nothing but a prelude to giving all of my people paradise within their lifetimes."

The American ambassador, Jack Holman, removed his sunglasses to squint at him. "Mr President, this is mighty impressive.

The Tomorrow Tower

If only the White House looked this good then maybe people would stop shooting at it."

"Indeed," Santari said, forcing a smile. He hated Americans. He thought Americans believed God was on their side, and everyone else should bow to their weapon superiority. Their god was money. Their religion was greed. He could taste bile each time he had to pretend to be friends with one. Santari's sources had bribed one of Jack Holman's aides, to find out the man's foibles: Holman had two mistresses and a secret Swiss bank account. Worse than the information he'd learned was the knowledge that Holman's aides were corruptible, for Santari prided himself on the loyalty of his staff. Without loyalty, he was nothing. Jack Holman was nothing.

He led the foreigners to a shaded table overlooking the gardens. Two loyal servants offered French Champagne - vintage 2006 - that they accepted greedily. Santari refrained, given his distaste for alcohol. He had found that Westerners relaxed under such circumstances, so he could talk business. A status feed implanted in his right eye read their biorhythms and informed him when they were suitably relaxed.

"My country is one of the top three natural oil producers in the world. However, geo-surveys have shown that in twenty years our wells will be dry." And, he thought grimly, it will take less time for nanoengineers to start producing oil unnaturally. He paused and watched the American's cool gaze. "I am a simple man, a man with no Oxford education, no blue blood in my veins, yet even I can see that unless something is done all I have struggled to create will vanish like water in the desert."

"I feel for you," Holman said.

Telltales read the ambassador's body language, informing Santari that the man was lying.

"My country needs overseas investments in technology that it is simply not receiving. The present arms embargo for so-called human rights infringements gets in the path of progress. Your countries benefit considerably from our oil, so I'm sure you would not wish for the situation to change."

The French ambassador coughed. "You desire a special arrangement?"

"I am only stating facts, Messier Pualac. Perhaps some of you can offer a solution?"

*

Santari signed Jack Holman's papers with his DNA signature and was surprised when Jack Holman frowned. "Something wrong?"

"Hell, the damn machine's not working. Lousy Japtech junk!" The ambassador strolled to the helicopter - no doubt to check the bank - and returned smiling. Already the millions would be in the ambassador's Swiss account, sent by a coded communication. Jack Holman was a tough negotiator; he required twice the bribe of the French and British. Now he held a box of Havanan cigars.

"I hear these are your favourite."

Santari grinned.

The Tomorrow Tower

"You are a truly decadent nation." *And I'd like to stamp on you with my foot.*

They shook hands and then Holman boarded the helicopter. Santari stepped back before the blades gathered speed. The ambassador waved as it lifted off, grinning.

Santari watched the helicopter fly over the Great Pyramid before he returned to his private chambers to thoroughly wash his hands.

He sensed someone in the doorway and reflexively grabbed the 9mm pistol beneath his jacket.

He calmed when he saw it was General Malawi.

"Yes?" He sounded not quite as forcible as he wished. "What is it?"

"Sir, are you ready to watch the executions?"

*

The executions made Santari desire a cigar to calm his nerves, but it tasted bitter and he stubbed it out in the limousine's ashtray. It reminded him of the burning buildings he'd looted as a boy, looking for food but finding bodies and blackened skeletons. The memory was not pleasant. "General, do I really like these cigars?"

"Sir? You love cigars."

"Then these are exceptionally poor."

He emptied the cigar case into the ashtray and watched them ionise. Then he concentrated on the closed palace gates and the cause of his worry, the people beyond them. A Molotov cocktail burst against the wall. Zarabian soldiers forced the angry crowd back, shooting offenders with biotags for later retribution. They opened the gates. Escort vehicles - bikes and rocket-launching APCs - moved ahead, followed by three black limousines identical to Santari's. Santari's own car went next, and then six more limousines followed. It was a precaution necessary for confusing any assassination attempts. Security was tight. He had heard a rumour that the rebels had a sample of his DNA and were planning a prion attack. They'd like nothing more than to give him kuru or CJD if they could hit him. Discreet, delayed assassinations were in fashion. Once the limousines were outside, they separated, going on fake routes.

Santari watched the ravaged city through the bulletglass while Malawi read out a summary of the casualties in the North. Many soldiers had died in squalid urban fighting, playing cat-and-mouse with the rebels, and it was his duty to improve morale with an impromptu visit to the front line - planned six weeks ago. He recalled how he had defeated the Communists by such a tactic. He would not fall into the same trap through neglect.

"Malawi, pull my armies out of rebel-infested cities and block all escape routes. I want it announced that unless the rebels surrender they will face airstrikes."

Malawi grinned. "Yes, sir!" He barked orders to the front lines via weblink. "What deadline should I give, sir?"

"Twenty-four hours. Then we bomb them."

The Tomorrow Tower

The limousine entered a tunnel and emerged in the twilight world of Santari's childhood. He looked through the windows with pain in his heart. Bleak concrete towers rose skyward like malignant melanomas, a cancer of the very land. Pro-democracy graffiti scourged stucco walls and defaced Government posters. Santari flashed an angry look at Malawi.

"The scourge infest my city!"

"Sir, I'll have the graffiti removed and investigated."

"Democracy doesn't work. Don't those idealist weaklings know that? The countries that purport to have democracy are no more than hegemonies for the wealthy upper-class. Strong leadership is essential. *My* leadership."

"Yes, sir."

Santari glimpsed dirty, hollow faces in the shadows of an abandoned hotel and thought he saw a familiar face. He almost ordered the driver to stop, but he hesitated.

He didn't know anyone in the outskirts.

The limousine passed a huge hologram of himself. His recorded voice was promising ever-lasting peace through strong leadership.

A young man stood under the holo, staring at the limo. Santari knew him. He recognised the scar on his jaw. But the name would not come. The man bent down and flashed a plastic lighter to something hidden in a paper bag, keeping his eyes focused on the limo.

"Kishtar?" Santari mumbled.

The Tomorrow Tower

The man's name was Kishtar.

Kishtar pitched the burning bag at Santari's limousine.

"Driver! Petrol bomb!"

Too late. The bottle burst open on the windscreen and engulfed it in flames. The driver braked urgently. Santari jolted forward and tasted blood in his mouth. The limo screamed to a controlled stop. He could hear small-arms fire and hear Malawi shouting something. Bullets dented the windows. Santari kept his head down beneath the seats while his security teams fired automatic weapons. The battle was brief. The rebels vanished into the derelict housing. When it was safe, he put his head up and looked around. His biochecks flashed green in his periphery optics. He'd suffered no injuries.

Soldiers swarmed over the street, dragging derelicts towards the ID vans for DNA checks and loyalty implants.

"Driver, move on now."

"Sir," Malawi said, "he's dead."

*

Santari could not sleep in his four-poster bed that night. He lay tangled in the silk sheets, sweating. Earlier he had angrily dismissed his concubines without an explanation even to himself as to his lack of desire. No, he was not angry for the reason his concubines suspected; he had accepted assassination attempts long ago as part of his life. He believed his enemies would fall, like the Communists had fallen. They could kill him, but he would not die. No, the assassination attempt did not bother him.

No, it was Kishtar.

A man he had never seen before, but someone he felt he knew. How did he know the man's name so positively?

Santari had not mentioned recognising Kishtar to his staff. He wondered why he was reluctant to tell them the name of the assassin when the man had tried to kill him. Perhaps the man had been on his staff years ago, and the memory engrams in his new body had simply not copied the information with 100% parity. Maybe. He'd studied the IDs of the dead rebels. Kishtar wasn't one of them. He could see Kishtar clearly in his mind, but younger, without the scar. He knew Kishtar's scar was from grenade shrapnel. How did he know the impossible?

He tried sleeping alone for the first time in the terrible months since the bombing, but he was restless.

That night haunted him.

He remembered sitting at the dining table, discussing state matters with his sons and generals. Drinking the finest wines. Eating Beluga caviar.

The waiter had slipped through the security net.

Santari had seen the explosives wrapped around his waist as he launched himself forward in the name of democracy. The generals panicked. His sons had stopped the man and thrown him to the ground, but then the bomb exploded. Santari had been the only one of twenty to be revived after the explosion, waking in the hospital without a scratch. His new body had already been given plastic surgery before he woke, so it was almost as though he had not been injured. He had always been lucky. His propaganda machine said he was the Son of God. He wondered if he was. Maybe that was his curse, to be divine in a world without faith.

He got out of bed and walked onto the balcony. He could hear the rapport of a machine gun somewhere in the night. Red and green tracer bullets lit the sky like fireworks. They reminded him of the celebrations three decades before when he had declared victory from the rooftop of the old palace, raising an AK-47 to the heavens.

It seemed so long ago.

Now he was hated for doing the things others could not. Who else could have reshaped the slums? Who else could feed all the people? Who else could give them schools and jobs? He had been born for greatness. He would not let it slip away. If history had taught him anything, it was that people soon forgot the good things and always remembered the bad. Democracy let the foolish and corrupt have power. It bred moral slackness and lethal procrastination. Society needed a strong government. It needed men like Santari. No one possessed his visions. His enemies had to be stamped out of existence.

He needed to destroy the Kishtars of the world.

He shuddered from the rage within him and stepped inside, balling his fists. Deep grief for his two sons rocked him. He had loved them so much that he had planned to step aside for them to rule.

"Why did you have to die, my sons?"

The Tomorrow Tower

His thoughts drifted to the most recent assassination attempt. He thought about Kishtar. It was odd. When he thought about the man, he felt the same way as he did for his sons. Slowly, the anger drained and was replaced by frustration. Why could he not remember how he knew the man? He felt weak. He could not even kill a man who wanted to kill him. Something was wrong with him.

Santari cried.

But the worst thing was he did not know why.

*

In one minute, the private subway train carried Santari from the palace to the bowels of the Great Pyramid. It stopped smoothly above where the chemical vats processed organo-halogens for chemical weapons. Walking along a gantry, Santari touched a vat. He could almost feel its deadly power. He continued through an airlock: BIOWEAPONS LEVEL 4. Only his top men and the research team had access to the room.

He looked through Plexiglas into a vacuum-sealed room, where canisters of Ebola virus waited. He'd had a team collect it from refuse sites in Zaire - digging up infected corpses.

Dr Raymond greeted him solemnly. "Mr President, I'm afraid once the virus is released it could spread further than the target zones."

"It's a risk I'm willing to take."

The scientist nodded.

The Tomorrow Tower

Santari's status feed showed the man was nervous.

He needs a loyalty implant, Santari thought, walking through the doors to the War Room.

The Ebola virus was a short-term purge, nothing a virologist couldn't combat given time. It was here in the War Room, a room paid for by Jack Holman and his like, where the real war would be won.

The doors closed behind him.

The generator was surprisingly small. He'd expected something a lot bigger than the pebbled-sized sphere. Switched on, the generator would manipulate vacuum energy. The risks were huge, but the rewards were infinite. He was the only man in the world with the resources to build it. He would be a god among men. His name would be written in the stars. And, he thought, what a weapon!

Just a few more pieces and he would be ready.

*

Santari turned away from the newslink and rubbed his tired eyes. The rebels had not surrendered - yet. Stubborn fools. He wasn't going to kill them. Didn't they know that? He'd give them the option of loyalty implants or death by firing squad. It wasn't as if they'd become zombies. Some of his best aides had the implants and they acted just like ordinary humans. In fact, he couldn't tell the difference unless he knew.

He walked onto the balcony, checking his weblink for

appointments. His next teleconference was in fifteen minutes. Time enough to call the name Kishtar up on his computer, which was something he'd delayed beyond the rational. He'd been putting it off with excuses, wanting to know who Kishtar was and yet fearing the answer.

He was disappointed by the number of entries. There were 10780. Kishtar was a popular name in the country. He isolated the search to the capital. Again, too many. He isolated it to the outskirts. Six names and addresses appeared ... one strangely familiar.

Proximity senses in his epidermis rippled. He switched off the computer and turned around. General Malawi had entered the room uninvited.

"General Malawi, I don't like to be disturbed."

"I am concerned about your health, sir. The internal security minister believes you may have suffered a shock after the attack. There has also been odd access to the web. Who is this Kishtar?"

"You have been monitoring me?" He faced Malawi and saw the man blanch. "You are spying on your own leader?"

"No, sir. Merely internal security. We're concerned about the integrity of your memory engrams. Are you suffering recall glitches?"

"Malawi, you are a pup strayed too far out of the kennel! Get out of my sight!"

"Yes, sir." The general shirked out of sight.

As soon as the general was gone, Santari ordered a security detail to sweep his room. The agents were guaranteed loyal through the latest hardware neuroplants. They found several nanoscopic bugs in and on the walls, even painted on a Picasso, and even logged onto his weblink.

Malawi called with an apology, saying he was worried about further assassinations and that was why he'd taken the precautions.

Santari didn't believe him.

It was part of a plot to kill him.

But he had to act as if he didn't know. He would deal with Malawi later. First, he headed to the TV studio on the 200th floor. He did his QNN interview, which he thought went excellently. Then headed to the Great Pyramid before his security guards arrived for his own *protection*.

He had to escape the assassination: Malawi would not wait now he was uncovered.

Santari stopped the train halfway. It slid to a halt at a ventilation node. He forced the door open with the manual wrench. A siren sounded far away. He ripped off his weblink and hurried along the tunnel and out into the gardens. The Great Pyramid dwarfed him, burnt sienna in the evening light. He ran across a lawn to the palm trees. A helicopter swooped over his head. A man in a black helmet leaned out of the side window.

"Please come back, Mr President!"

Santari pulled out his pistol, steadied his aim and fired. The body slumped and tumbled. The helicopter - a personnel carrier with no weapons system - veered towards the palace while the body hit the ground.

The Tomorrow Tower

Santari hurried to the body and stripped the dead soldier of his uniform. He felt strangely powerful sliding on the armour, suddenly becoming anonymous. Tactical readouts fed in from the VR. Until he knew the extent of the infiltration of his command, he could trust no one but himself.

He slipped out of the main gates as one of a crowd of night patrol officers. He separated from the group and hijacked a truck, driving to the outskirts. Telltales showed he was being chased. An impulse told him to find Kishtar, possibly his only loyal subject.

*

Twenty years earlier, the building had been a block of family units. He stopped the truck in the forecourt, pooling dust as the hydrofoils slowed and died. He jumped out and pulled his pistol. He felt deja vu pulling open the door leading up into the darkness. He climbed the stairs until he was on the fourth floor, out of breath. The man he was looking for was Kishtar Nahubi, last known address number 405. Looking at the empty apartments, he knew the whole place was deserted.

Except? Except he had to go on.

Something was compelling him onward.

He reached apartment 405, scanning for movement. It was bare. Concrete mites had eaten away at the floor, the rogue nanos the product of a Chinese factory that had released a defective batch some thirty years back. He stepped inside the main room, passing the empty kitchen and bedroom, and walked carefully to the boarded-up windows. He pulled a board loose to allow the city to flood the dark corners in yellow light.

He knew this room.

He had grown up here.

He had seen the birth of his only child in this room.

His only son.

Kishtar.

Something whined in his skull.

He fell to his knees, clutching his head. He removed the helmet. The pain was incredible. I'm having a stroke, he thought. I'm having a stroke. But the pain receded … and he was left staring at a string of blood coming out of his nose – blood that didn't want to stop. A metal pin fell out and hit the concrete.

A loyalty implant.

He - Santari - had a loyalty implant.

His own people had not trusted his memory engrams in a new body and mind.

He staunched the bleeding and staggered to his feet.

He wasn't Santari.

He was Roual Nahubi, the father of Kishtar Nahubi.

And he remembered *everything*.

Twenty years had passed since he had hidden his boy under the floor, so Santari's soldiers could not take him away for loyalty implanting. As a young man, Kishtar had been in a crowd of protesters when a grenade landed. Roual had seen the shrapnel scar his son's face. He had tended to the wound.

After the protest, Santari had demanded the rounding up of the protesters, including his son. A relative had taken Kishtar in while he recovered. Santari's men arrested Roual instead, did things to him, left him in prison, forgotten. But his physical similarities to the great leader had been noted.

One day, they had come for him. They took him to a special place – a secret operating room.

Without anaesthetic, rubber-masked surgeons had adjusted him to a facsimile of Santari. Santari had been on the operating table beside him – dead. Too much damage for a total brain transplant. A neuroplant engramming was all the scared military officers could do in the time available.

They needed Santari alive to keep themselves in power.

They had made Roual into Santari.

But now he remembered his real name.

Roual was so confused he did not hear the man creeping up on him.

"Hands up, Mr President."

He obeyed.

"Face me."

Kishtar was standing two strides away. Fresh blood seeped out of a leg wound. He had a Mac-10 pointed at his father's chest. "This used to be my home. Then you took my father away for *questioning*."

Roual paled. "My son? It's me! Your father! Roual!"

Kishtar stared at him, looking into his eyes. Roual could tell he saw something in them that caused his weapon to waver. Santari heard footsteps from above. Kishtar looked up, frowning. Roual could hear a helicopter. He realised his access to the web must have given Internal Security the address. He had led them here. "Listen to me. I am your father!"

Kishtar was shaking. "You're not my father. You lie!"

"Santari used me! He grafted his memories into me, but the surgeons left parts of my personality intact because they couldn't erase them. His men needed a loyalty implant to keep me behaving like him. Look at the floor! Don't you see it?"

Kishtar looked at the loyalty implant. "That was in you?"

"Yes!"

"Father, I thought you were dead."

"I might as well be," Roual said.

Kishtar aimed the gun. "I can't take the chance they can use you, Father. Santari must die!"

Roual spread his arms, offering himself. He wanted to die. It was justice. He had lived as the traitor. It was right his son should kill him.

"Do it!" he cried.

A burst of gunfire lit the room.

Roual saw Kishtar's chest ripple and open, spraying crimson meat. He toppled. Soldiers stormed into the room.

Kishtar was dead. His eyes continued to stare, accusing. His face slackened and became still and lifeless.

Roual wanted to weep for his son, but he forced himself to look calm and reveal nothing of his inner turmoil.

The Tomorrow Tower

General Malawi rushed into the room. "Are you are all right, Mr President?"

"Yes," Roual said, quickly stepping on the implant to crush it into the dust. "Yes, I'm fine."

*

Roual looked at the Great Pyramid and thought of its contents. The Ebola virus was just the beginning of the end. He had he really believed he was ready to use vacuum energy without trials, safety precautions and controls? He could taste Santari's thoughts still in his mind, as if they had coated him in corruption and madness.

Ancient B-52s, surplus bombers bought off Jack Holman, rumbled across the skyline carrying their lethal payload.

General Malawi strolled onto the balcony. "I am glad to see you are feeling better, sir."

Roual nodded. He'd persuaded the general he'd decided on a personal search for the assassin, and, with no knowledge of the failed loyalty implant, the general had no reason not to believe. Roual could play the part of Santari and no one would ever know. He possessed Santari's memories, but he was no longer controlled by them. But when he thought of Kishtar dying and Santari's sons dying, the feelings mixed and twisted and fermented in his stomach. He was sick of the regime. Santari had hated the Americans, but he did not. Santari's pyramid was an offence to nature. Roual would not destroy the world.

"The deadline's gone, sir. Should I give the order?"

"No, General."

The Tomorrow Tower

"Sir?"

"What would you do if you thought I was not myself anymore?"

"I don't know what you mean, sir."

"The engrams failed, General. That's why I don't like cigars. The *real* me doesn't smoke. I'm just some poor victim. You could never make me into that vial abomination you call a leader."

Malawi reached for his weblink, but he stopped when Roual raised his pistol.

"Tell me the truth. Why did you do it?"

"We needed a great leader, sir. When you died, we did what we could to save your memories. We used a prisoner and gave him extensive surgery and implanted your mind as best as we could."

"I know that. But why?"

"You are the man who keeps this country together, sir. With no leader, everything will be lost. We need firm guidance and your vision. Don't you understand that?"

"I understand perfectly. It has to end."

"Pardon, sir?"

"It must end!"

Roual shot Malawi in the temple. Malawi was so surprised he stood there for several seconds until he flopped over the balcony. Roual watched the body land in the grass.

He opened his weblink to Security.

"Open the palace gates," he said, knowing their loyalty implants would force them to obey. "Let the people in."

For once, Roual thought, Santari would be a true hero.

WAVES ON A DISTANT SHORE

After the car crash that killed his wife and baby daughter, David Bachman's dreams were like road signs on a fog-bound motorway. He glimpsed strange things, but they were gone before his mind could recognise them. He would wake in the hospital bed *knowing* there was something vital his unconsciousness was trying to tell him, which was more disconcerting than no dreams at all. Instinctively, he knew that remembering the dreams would have dire consequences, giving him the directions to a place he did not want to go.

Once David's broken bones had recovered, he went back to teaching English at Fenchley Comprehensive School, mostly to have his mind occupied with work, to blank out the pain of loss, but his mind didn't feel right. It was as though he and the rest of the world were running at different speeds. Like the purple scar on his cheek,

182

The Tomorrow Tower

his mind would not heal, not fully. He was in a loop of denial and remembrance. Any time of day or night he would see the red smear of the drunk driver's rear lights and be transported there, in the car, as it was happening. Suddenly braking on the infinite road. Desperately clawing at the wheel. Melissa crying out his name in sheer panic, as if he could do something, anything. The tree. The bushes. The rocks. The impact. The explosion. He should have reacted faster. Should have ... what?

His fear of the dreams grew with each night until he could not sleep more than minutes at a time. He would be suddenly sitting bolt-upright, his heart palpitating, reaching for a wife who was no longer there. Then he would lie down again and attempt to sleep. Eyes closed, pressure-sense Rorschach patterns painted his eyelids. Inkblot studies into madness. He could almost see human faces in the patterns. But just as he thought he was about to see something important, the sea of nightmares would seep away. He could almost see Rachel and Melissa, two X-ray skeletons, their jawbones moving silently, calling him. Needing him. But he didn't want to join them in the blackness. The blackness was death.

Death was not the way. He didn't want to die. So he kept himself awake with coffee and cigarettes and late-night TV. A terrible self-enforced insomnia ruled the darkness. Sleep eluded him as if he were trying to grip an electric eel. Staying awake was just as painful as succumbing to sleep, tiredness draining the colour out of his days.

He was going crazy.

The Tomorrow Tower

The human mind required REM sleep to function, or thoughts would build up like lava in a volcanic vent, exploding in a psychotic episode. This he knew; this he could feel. The pressure building up in his head was incredible. In the English lessons he taught, pupils started asking what was wrong with sir; he seemed so distant. He was so tired and irritable that he could not focus on the teaching. They assumed it was only the tragedy - that drunk driver, the loss of his family - plaguing his thoughts. But even his thoughts seemed alien. Weird. Somehow *imposed* from somewhere else.

Then came the visions.

He could look at his students and see fleeting images, like tracing paper over a drawing.

The world *behind* the real world.

It was 3.11 p.m. - four minutes to go before the final lesson ended - when the world he knew and believed in shattered.

One second he was telling everyone to pack up their books, and the next he could see ... everything.

*

Strange funnels of rainbow light snaked between his students, joining and entwining, sprouting loops and limbs. They were all connected, some connected with vast pulsating tubes, like bunched fibre optic cables, some connected with smaller ones, diaphanous cobwebs. Those students he knew were best friends had the thickest connections. Teenage romances were thick knots of rainbow light.

The Tomorrow Tower

As students looked around, picking up their books, snaking coils passed out of them and into others, blue-white flashes like sparks from a Van de Graaff generator. David could see flirting glances as red lasers. A girl with a supposedly secret crush on him bathed him in a crimson light.

Then the vision vanished, leaving him wondering if it had happened at all.

Had his brain been damaged in the crash? If so, how come the MRI scans had shown nothing? The doctors wouldn't have released a madman, would they?

"D-dismissed," he said, and watched his students leave.

*

"David," said the headteacher in the second week of the term, "you need to take more time off."

"Time off ..." An aura danced out of the headteacher's head. An electric Medusa. Couldn't he see it?

"I lost my own wife to cancer, so I know how you feel." David could *see* how he felt, too. Black and grey spikes coursed through his hair. "It's worse than losing a leg. You need to sort things out in your mind."

"Sort things out." David nodded. He wasn't ready to come back to work. And he definitely needed to sort out his mind. He could see his bones through his skin and the blood flowing in his veins. "Thanks."

"Get yourself well, David. Don't worry about the job. It'll always be here for you. Take a holiday in the sun. Spain's nice this time of year. That's where the kids go when they should be at school." The headteacher paused. A green cone of concern leapt out of him, striking David, moving like a tornado over his skin. It was oddly beautiful, bringing tears. "And if that doesn't help, I know a good psychiatrist you could talk to."

"Psychiatrist?"

"She specialises in bereavement counselling. Her name's Joyce Benson."

I need more than a psychiatrist, David thought. His thought was a black ribbon blowing in a breeze.

*

He did not see the psychiatrist. A sympathetic doctor with purple flutes shimmering out of his hands wrote a barbiturate prescription to help him sleep, but as soon as David was home he realised he could not take the sleeping pills. Pills may have given him the blankness of enforced sleep, but what if he dreamt the dream and remembered it? What then? No, he could not risk it. First, he needed to understand this phenomenon, why this thing was happening, what it meant, why dreaming filled him with dread, and why he could see things which were not there.

He dressed in jeans and a T-shirt to pass himself off as a post-graduate student and went to his local university library. Surrounded by undergraduates with giant coronas coming out of their heads, coronas brightening to supernovas each time they read something enlightening, he looked for answers.

Psychology texts didn't help much, just telling him he had a problem, so he turned to other subjects: medicine, philosophy, cosmology, religion ... and mathematics. Why he was drawn to the mathematics section was then a mystery; he'd never liked the subject at school, never mind *understood* it. After all, he taught English for a reason. But now he was drawn there.

The dusty shelves looked like they'd never been touched. But leafing through the red leather-bound hardbacks, he saw things starting to fall into place. Computer-produced fractal images looked exactly like some of the patterns he'd seen at 4 a.m. behind his eyelids. Then he read about Fourier waves and topology and geometry and ... though he didn't understand many of the symbols and equations, he knew he was onto something. As he pored over text after text, reading, reading, reading, his jigsaw knowledge started assembling itself, becoming whole.

There was a theory in a physics journal that knotted his stomach and sent his head pounding.

M-theory.

Apparently, M-theory could be the "Theory of Everything", if it was solved. He pored over the article with deepening concern.

He was carrying a pile of books to a desk when he noticed one student wasn't emitting any strange light. Shimmering threads entered her, but none were being produced. Why? There was only one thing different. She was asleep.

He was looking at her when his mind wandered. And something

The Tomorrow Tower

forced its way into his mind. Seeing the sleeping student triggered a mental reaction.

He had a waking dream.

*

In his dream, he was standing on a white beach with a rocky shore, looking out at the ocean. The waves were coming in, huge breakers exploding against the rocks with extreme violence. He could feel the cold spray hit his face from the safety of the sand. After each wave receded there was something new washed up on the shore - a car tyre, a steering wheel, a rusty exhaust pipe ... parts of his wrecked car ... and then there were two bodies, Rachel and Melissa, rolling over in the wet sand. They were alive. He heard them call to him.

He ran towards them, but a second wave rose up and engulfed them, submerging them in its icy water. He dived into the wave, swimming as hard as he could. But the wave disappeared, leaving him floundering on the empty beach. The waves continued, but they deposited nothing more on the sand. Rachel and Melissa had been dragged back into the ocean.

On the horizon, there was a black line separating sky and ocean that had not been there before. The line was widening. It was a wave, a vast wall of water, a tidal wave longer and higher than he thought possible. It was powering towards the beach. He looked around. There was no way of escape because the beach ended at a cliff. The tidal wave roared, pushing a cold wind ahead of it. It was coming closer and closer to the shore. A perfectly vertical wall of darkness.

He ran. The shadow soon fell on him. It would drown him and crush him and squash him against the cliff. He screamed.

The waking dream dissolved before his eyes.

*

The student had woken up at his scream. She was looking at him as though he were a pervert. Dark green concern flayed out of her head and quickly changed to red anger. He left hurriedly.

*

Outside the university he suddenly understood his problem. And it scared him, for what he learnt was a revelation as large as the universe.

His dreaming was dangerous, and it was connected to his reading about M-theory. M-theory was an attempt by theoretical physicists to create a simple theory that explained the universe. It was an extension of superstring theory, overcoming the problems of that theory and going far beyond. M-theory had many solutions, and only one fitted the universe. In M-theory, there were eleven dimensions, with the familiar four experienced by humans just the surface of a deeper reality. He was *seeing* those dimensions. And if he dreamt the solution, he would cease to exist, winked out of existence.

189

The Tomorrow Tower

He needed help desperately because he believed his own crazy theory.

So that was why he ended up in the pink carpeted office of Dr Joyce Benson, staring at the psychiatrist through his black-ringed and bloodshot eyes. He was relieved that his visions had stopped for a moment. The world had returned to its solid three-dimensional self. He smoked cigarette after cigarette. The leather chair creaked under him. The black couch was the only item in the room that fitted his stereotype expectations, and he'd chosen not to use it. Everything else could have been in a hotel suite. A large window poured light in through the pink blinds. Van Gogh's *Sunflowers* hung on the wall. A bad choice, he thought, since the artist went insane with syphilis. There was no desk, no "ego wall" packed with certificates and awards. A dictation machine whirred on the coffee table between them, recording the silence. The pink room said *friendly*.

"I haven't been to a psychiatrist before," David said. He regretted his tone immediately; it implied he was above visiting a psychiatrist. He didn't feel that way. Maybe it was all in his head. Deluded people thought bizarre things were real. That was how you knew they were deluded. Sanity was just a consensus vote.

Joyce Benson tapped her notepad with her fountain pen. She offered a grandmotherly smile. "Most people who visit a psychiatrist aren't crazy, you know."

"They aren't? I mean, I don't suppose they are."

"The crazy ones get seats in the Houses of Parliament and make the rules."

The Tomorrow Tower

He laughed uneasily. A political psychiatrist. Great.

"Relax, David. I'm not a Freudian. I don't ask questions about your mother."

"She's dead," he said, surprising himself with the harshness in his tone. "The dreams killed her."

Shouldn't have said that, he thought. *Why did I say that? Now she'll know I'm a nut. Listen to me, talking to myself. Nut, nut, nut. You're a nut, that's what you are. They could packet you and sell you in pubs.* But he knew that it was true: his mother had killed herself because of the dreams. She'd died when he was a baby, but now focusing on it made him remember her as if her suicide had happened yesterday.

"I have to stop the thoughts in my head," she had said, leaning over his cot, kissing him gently. Then she had gone away forever: a bottle of aspirins had done it.

"What was that you said?" the psychiatrist asked.

It is a hereditary problem, David realised. The accident did not cause the hallucinations. The accident and the bereavement had merely triggered his mind into a different way of perceiving reality, unleashing some hidden talent stored in his genes.

The psychiatrist leant forward, putting the notepad aside.

She said something.

"Pardon?" he said. His thoughts were too loud, like tinnitus, muffling the sounds of the external world.

"I said you don't have to talk about anything that makes you uncomfortable. I won't write anything down if it helps. Please, David, I suggest you tell me what you want from these sessions. Be as complete as you can."

"I've been having these dreams," he said, and told her what she would accept, including the glimpses of another world, but stopping his story at the point before he visited the university library. He needed to trust her before he told her the results of his research. He concluded: "I need to prevent this dream from coming through from the dark place. I know it sounds vague, but I assure you the feeling I get is very real and very scary."

"Insomnia is often a manifestation of a deeper problem," she said. "Fear of sleep is unusual, but not unique. Obviously, the sudden deaths of your family have deeply hurt you. Such a stressor can do more harm than you can imagine. Do you fear that by going to sleep and having this dream, you will die in the dream - and consequently die in real life?"

"Yes, but it's worse than that."

"Worse than death?"

"Definitely."

The dictation machine clicked off. He'd been talking for thirty minutes. Dr Benson ejected the cassette and flipped it over. She made two coffees before resuming the session.

"What's worse than death?" she asked.

"An absence of everything. A void of absolute nothing. At least with death the person is remembered by those still living, but this ... this thing in my dream transcends death. This dream is the sum of the whole universe, positives and negatives cancelling out everything, breaking down the symmetries that everything is built upon. It's nothing in all meanings of the word. And if I dream it, it will become real." He was sweating as if he'd been running a marathon. It dripped off his forehead and onto the pink carpet, where it stained like blood. Do I sound crazy? Yes. Do I sound like a madman ranting at a brick wall? Yes. Am I crazy? No.

"A dream can't alter the universe," she said.

I do sound crazy.

"I've been researching it," he admitted. "I have a theory. It probably sounds like pure fantasy, but I need someone to listen."

"I'm listening, David. Whatever you say will remain confidential. Now, what's your theory?"

"Don't you ever feel that things happen because they have to happen?"

"Everyone feels that some days."

"Exactly. Call it fate or destiny or whatever; it looks like things have been set up so they happen in a specific way." Like the car crash, he thought, wiping acid sweat out of his eyes. "I don't believe in coincidences anymore. Things happen because they *have* to happen. Things might not make sense - they don't have to because nobody is writing the rules - but there are always the hidden laws. The Laws of the Waves."

"Waves?"

"The universe is made out of nothing but energy waves," he said.

Dr Benson looked puzzled. She had a right; the picture was only coming clear to him as he talked it through. He told her about his waking dream. "I think the whole thing was a metaphor. The beach was reality, where I am. The ocean was the imagination, the unconscious. The waves were where these places overlap. When I tried to reach Rachel and Melissa, I failed because they no longer exist. But I kept trying to reach them, but the water rejected me. Then there was the tidal wave, which probably symbolised the end of everything. It was so dark and endless."

He shuddered at the memory.

"David, what do you think will happen if the tidal wave had reached you?"

"I think the universe would have stopped existing."

"Interesting. Tell me more."

David could feel the room changing, or, rather, his *perception* of the room. It happened fast. Unnamed colours streamed in through the windows, the walls fading to a transparent veneer. He could see through objects. Dr Benson leant forward, her face emitting a bright cherry glow, her fingers shimmering with a vermilion light.

"What do you see?" she said.

"I see ... your words coming out of your mouth like raindrops splashing on a still lake. I can see the air molecules moving towards me as they make a sound wave. The colours are like ... nothing I've seen before. My God, it's amazing. I can hear some music - no, radio waves, I think. Yes, there are radio waves raining down from the sky, and I can hear them, all signals at once, voices, songs. If I concentrate very hard, I can listen to just one at a time."

"David?"

The Tomorrow Tower

He felt someone touching his shoulder. The contact collapsed his vision. The room conformed to familiarity.

"For a moment you looked spellbound," Dr Benson said.

"I was. It's an awesome experience."

"It's only a hallucination, David."

"No."

"I'm afraid so."

"But I could see so much."

"It's a condition called synaesthesia. That's when someone can hear what they see or see what they hear. Drugs like LSD can cause it or it can happen perfectly naturally. Some artists and musicians have it. Some people can hear a word and think, say, the colour pink, and whenever they hear the same word, it's the same pink every time. Apart from that, they live perfectly normal lives, as can you. I'll admit that for someone to have the condition in a latent capacity is unheard of, but combined with the stress of losing your family in so brutal a way, the synaesthesia has manifested itself just as your present emotional difficulties are at a peak. At the heart of your problem is your trouble adapting to the world without Rachel and Melissa. You have to accept their deaths, David."

"I don't think so," he said. "No offence - I think you're completely wrong. This *hallucination* switches itself on and off with a purpose. What I can see isn't imaginary! It's real! More real than what you see as you talk to me. Excuse me, but I have to go."

"We haven't finished the session -"

"I'm sorry," he mumbled. He hurried outside, through the

reception area and towards his car. He was feeling his pockets for his keys when Dr Benson entered the car park.

"David, I want to help you."

"You don't believe me."

"I believe it's real to you. That's what counts. Come inside and we can continue."

He paused, considering.

"I never explained my theory about the Laws of Waves."

"So come inside and tell me."

*

"What does that have to do with energy waves?" she said.

"I'll come to that, but I'll have to start at the beginning, with my research. First, you know how sound can be thought of as a wave?" She nodded, so he continued. "Well, with sound you can hear a piece of music that gets in your head and suddenly everyone is humming it, even if they hate it, right?"

"Yes."

"The sound waves make patterns in your mind, and your mind plays it over and over. It's as if the music has transmitted its essential essence, stored itself. But what creates the music? Another *mind*. Music is just an energy wave formed by vibrating molecules, but it can make you feel direct emotions. Why is that? It's because your consciousness is a similar sort of wave: more complicated, yes, but basically your soul is just a wave in more dimensions. *I can see those dimensions.*"

"I see," she said.

Do you? He doubted it. "It's impossible to describe what I see because it is constantly changing, but I believe each conscious entity from humans to amoebas possesses an identity, a special wave - or soul - unique to them that forms part of the fabric of the universe. It's as though the entire universe is just one big mathematical equation with our reality as one possible answer. Each soul is a part of the big equation, moving like a bead on an abacus towards the final solution. *And my dream is the solution to all the smaller equations put together.*"

"My maths is a bit fuzzy," the psychiatrist said. "What do you mean? In English?"

"Have you ever read *The Hitchhiker's Guide to the Galaxy*?"

"Yes, a long time ago. So?"

"In that story, the people ask a great computer to find the answer to the ultimate question. After years and years of calculating, it comes up with the answer: 42. But the answer is meaningless unless the question is known. The answer can't be in the same universe as the question. That might be a joke by Douglas Adams, but this is not. My dreams are getting closer and closer to the answer to everything! Then our real world will collapse to nothing. I can feel it, like a thickening in the atmosphere, a feeling of impending doom."

"I don't sense anything."

"Some people are closer to reaching the solution. My mother

was one. She almost reached the answer. But she killed herself to save the universe, even if she didn't understand why. I'm like her, approaching the answer. My dream will unravel the universe. I know it sounds crazy, but it's true. I'm not making it up. When I see things, I see emotions. I see the strings that bond us all together. The closer I get to the solution the clearer the universe becomes to me, and it scares the hell out of me."

He sat back, exhausted. The chair was glued to his hot buttocks.

"As you said earlier, David, it's just fantasy."

"But the patterns are becoming visible!" He stood up, no longer able to sit still. Why wouldn't she believe him? Was her mind so closed to new perceptions? He walked to the window. The sky broiled with grey clouds. The shapes were fractals, repeating patterns written in mathematical formulae. "Wait! I can prove it. The patterns show me things."

"David, you're becoming manic -"

He giggled, uncontrolled laughter slipping out. "It's happening again." He could see his own body patterns: blood, flesh and bone. Even the helices of DNA, vibrating. And smaller still - atoms and quarks and the nothingness between. The sight seemed to suck at his eyes, pulling him in. He had to force himself to look away, to look at Dr Benson. He could see her thoughts now, her inner voice, her identity. It was a beautiful band of silver and gold.

"Your life is a pattern, Doctor. I can see the strands coming out of you. I can see your past and your future. You are twice divorced, both times the men had affairs with younger women. You have a pet

The Tomorrow Tower

Labrador called Shelley, named after your favourite poet. You're a vegetarian and donate money to animal charities. You really wish you had married your childhood sweetheart, Henry, but you never told him how you felt. "

"How - how do you know that? Have you been stalking me?"

"You wanted children, but a complication after an ectopic pregnancy resulted in the removal of your womb. You deeply regret the loss and devote your time to helping others partly out of guilt, blaming yourself despite it being not your fault."

"My God -"

"And you live in a small village in a stone cottage. The roof is leaking and you promise you'll get it fixed, but -"

"Have you been watching me?"

"No. *No!* I can see your entire life. It's like a map, all written out. I know your life because your soul is clearly visible."

"I don't believe this," she said. A grey torus of disbelief wrapped around her like a doughnut. It started to shrink the more details of her life he told. "Okay, okay, I believe you!"

She was telling the truth, he saw.

At last, he had convinced someone.

He was weeping. "What can I do?"

"If it's really like an equation you are solving, I can see just two ways to stop yourself from solving it. The first way is to stop the calculator by killing yourself. I don't advocate that method. The other way is to make the equation unsolvable."

"How do I do that?"

The Tomorrow Tower

"Change the parameters."

Change the parameters.

He had to change the rules.

Death was a constant. But what if he could change it?

What if he could make Rachel and Melissa exist again?

David closed his eyes. If he pictured them hard enough, real enough, then they would be alive - in his universe. And if they existed, none of this would have happened. It would become just a dream. If he looked back in time and grabbed hold with both hands and willed him back to a time before the accident ... yes!

It sounded so simple.

It sounded impossible.

"I have to face the dream," he said.

Joyce Benson's head brightened as if a torch was shining out of her mouth and eyes and ears.

"I'll help you," she said. "Move over to the couch."

He did so.

"Lie down," she said. "Close your eyes."

Even with his lids shut, the world was just as vividly visible. He could see through the ceiling and through the clouds and beyond. A billion stars lit his sky with dizzying brightness, an optical overload. He could even see the nebulous splashes of alien thoughts on alien worlds.

"Relax," Joyce Benson said, sounding far away. "I'm going to hypnotise you."

His head pressed against the headrest, the full gravity of endless wakefulness weighing him down. The psychiatrist's reassuring voice kept him from panicking as the Rorschach patterns formed the faces of the dead. If only he could see Rachel and Melissa again. Alive.

He could see Joyce Benson standing over him, holding his pale hand as she induced a hypnotic state with quiet words. Instead of slipping into the abyss that waited for him, roller-coasting into non-existence, he controlled his descent towards the dream like an abseiler dropping off a cliff.

*

He was on the beach again.

He could no longer see Joyce Benson, but he could feel her presence like the warm hand of a mother.

The dream started where it had finished, the tidal wave mere seconds behind him. He faced it. The tidal wave loomed over his fragile body, but he wasn't afraid. When the wave reached him he embraced it and stared deep into the torrent, and let it swallow him whole.

Layer after layer of reality peeled away, like adding colour filters over a photograph. What remained was black and white. The blackness was the absence of everything: the death of the universe. The whiteness was the sum of love and truth and beauty and charm and strangeness. Fundamentals. He just had to choose a direction, a new way of looking, a new way of thinking.

He could change things.

The Tomorrow Tower

And with that thought, he took a giant mental leap. He rode a great tunnel of white light towards a distant shore. He knew where he was going. There, Rachel and Melissa still lived. The car crash had never happened. Dr Joyce Benson had children. And the universe had a purpose, and that purpose was good. Time and space were just variables in the big equation. He had the power to change them for the better.

And he did.

*

Joyce Benson blinked. She had a migraine. Nauseous waves of pain rolled over her. One second there had been a man on her couch, the next he had disappeared. The pain stopped as suddenly as it began. She felt as if the universe had shifted, somehow, corrected an anomaly.

Her office was empty. She was staring at a couch with no one lying there. Weird. She touched her swollen stomach, where her baby daughter kicked, eager to join her two grown-up brothers in the real world. At fifty, she had been surprised she could still have babies, but the unexpected pregnancy had been a miracle, a new lease of life. A strange feeling lingered as if she had not been pregnant until this very moment.

That was ridiculous. But yet ... hadn't she been talking with someone?

No. She had no appointments for the rest of the day. She

The Tomorrow Tower

decided to go home.

Henry would be missing her.

Her phone rang.

"Dr Benson speaking," she said.

"Thanks, Joyce," said a voice she did not know.

She could hear a child in the background, laughing.

"Pardon? Who is this?"

"Your guardian angel," the man said, hanging up.

Curiously, she believed him.

John Moralee © 2015

ABOUT THE AUTHOR

John Moralee lives in England, where his short fiction has appeared in magazines and anthologies including *The Mammoth Book of Jack the Ripper Stories*, *Clockwork Cairo*, and the British Fantasy Society's magazine. His novels and anthologies are available as Kindle ebooks and paperbacks.

BOOKS BY JOHN MORALEE

Acting Dead – a Rhode Island mystery novel

Journal of the Living – a British zombie apocalypse novel

Crowning Achievements: Legend of King Arthur – comic fantasy novel

The Bone Yard and Other Stories – horror short stories

Bloodways – horror short stories

The Quick and the Dread – horror short stories

Under Dark Skies – five crime stories with twists

Edge of Crime – crime fiction collection

The Good Soldier – short stories

The Tomorrow Tower – SF short stories

The Uncertainty Principle – SF short stories

Future Imperfect – SF stories

ANTHOLOGIES INCLUDING SHORT FICTION:

Visions III: Beyond the Kuiper Belt

Visions IV: Deep Space

Visions V: Milky Way

Visions VI: Galaxies

The Mammoth Book of Future Cops

The Mammoth Book of Jack the Ripper Stories

Hideous Progeny: A Frankenstein Anthology

Crimewave #1

Crimewave #2

Crimewave #3

Clockwork Cairo – a steampunk anthology including stories by Gail Carriger, Nisi Shawl, Chaz Brenchley and many others.

THANK YOU FOR BUYING THIS BOOK!

Printed in Great Britain
by Amazon